Advance Praise for *The Mirror*

"Lynn Freed is the absolute master of one of the great themes of contemporary life—a woman's ascent toward strength and self-definition. Funny thing is, her narratives are timeless and universal and transcending, and *The Mirror* is probably the most clear-eyed novel you'll read this year. This is what I want from a book, from a writer, and from a passionate heart."

BOB SHACOCHIS, author of *Easy in the Islands*

"A woman in full possession of her powers is a thrilling sight, and the powerful woman at the center of *The Mirror* conducts her life on her own unequivocal terms. The results are surprising and erotic, rendered in brisk, mordant prose by a writer with no interest in half measures."

AMY HEMPEL, author of *Tumble Home*

"In prose as precise and alluring as a spray of diamonds, *The Mirror* traces a remarkable woman's saga. It's a sexy, compelling, highly original retelling of Pygmalion, only in Lynn Freed's extraordinary novel, the narrator is both clay and sculptor, muse and visionary, a true heroine of her own making."

JILL CIMENT, author of *Half a Life*

"A credible voice that never strikes the wrong tone. Sparse and hard-eyed, shrewd without being cynical, *The Mirror* is an engaging tale, masterfully told."

IRINI SPANIDOU, author of *God's Snake*

"Lynn Freed has the remarkable ability to move her readers even as she compels them to think. *The Mirror's* heroine, Agnes La Grange, is the sort of woman we all long to be: strong yet warm, intelligent and independent, passionate yet nevertheless fierce in her requirements for love. The story of the consequences of those requirements creates a lesson in the nature of love itself. The novel is a surprisingly modern feminist parable—yet Freed's lyricism banishes any possibility of didacticism and keeps the characters superbly human. In its setting of sepia photographs and elegant design, *The Mirror* is as exquisite to hold as it is to read."

LINDA GRAY SEXTON, author of *Searching for Mercy Street: My Journey Back to My Mother, Anne Sexton* and *Points of Light*

THE MIRROR

Also by Lynn Freed

THE BUNGALOW

HOME GROUND

HEART CHANGE

THE MIRROR

A NOVEL

LYNN FREED

Crown Publishers, Inc.
New York

Published by Crown Publishers, Inc., 201 East 50th Street, New York, New York 10022. Member of the Crown Publishing Group.

Random House, Inc. New York, Toronto, London, Sydney, Auckland
http://www.randomhouse.com/

CROWN and colophon are trademarks of Crown Publishers, Inc.

Printed in the United States of America

Design by Nancy Kenmore

Library of Congress Cataloging-in-Publication Data
Freed, Lynn.
    The mirror / Lynn Freed. — 1st ed.
    1. Women—South Africa—Fiction.   I. Title.
    PR9369.3.F68M57   1997
    823 — dc21   97-265

ISBN 0-517-70320-3

10 9 8 7 6 5 4 3 2 1

First Edition

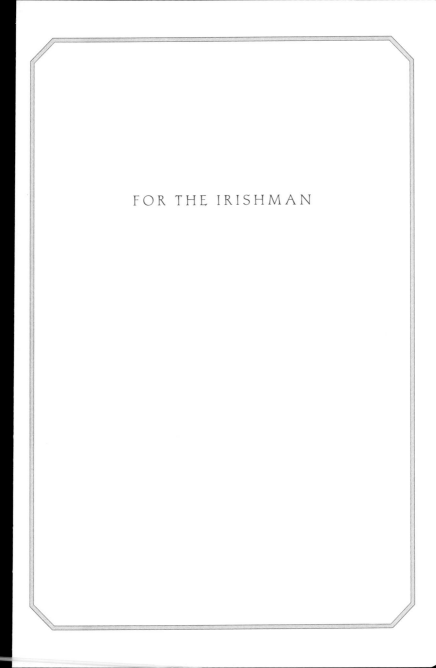

FOR THE IRISHMAN

SO WE'LL GO NO MORE A-ROVING

So we'll go no more a-roving
So late into the night,
Though the heart be still as loving,
And the moon be still as bright.

For the sword outwears its sheath,
And the soul wears out the breast,
And the heart must pause to breathe,
And Love itself have rest.

Though the night was made for loving,
And the day returns too soon,
Yet we'll go no more a-roving
By the light of the moon.

LORD BYRON

THE MIRROR

The house by the racecourse

1

I CAME INTO THAT HOUSE OF SICKNESS just after the Great War, as a girl of seventeen. They were there waiting for me, father and daughter, like a pair of birds, with their long noses and their great black eyes. The girl was a slip of a thing, no more than twelve, but she spoke up for the father in a loud, deep voice. Can you do this, Agnes? Have you ever done that? And the old man sat in his armchair with his watch chain and his penny spectacles, his pipe in his mouth and the little black moustache. Sometimes he said something to the girl in their own language, and then she would start up again. Agnes, do you know how to——

The wife was dying in the front parlor. They had moved a bed in there for her, and they kept the curtains drawn. In the lamplight, she looked a bit like a Red Indian, everything wide about her—eyes, mouth, nostrils, cheekbones. Even the hair was parted in the middle and pulled back into a plait.

From the start, she couldn't stand the sight of me. She would ring her little bell, and then, if I came in, give out one of her coughs, drawing the lips back from the raw gums to spit. And if that didn't do the trick, she growled and clawed her hands. So I had to call the native girl to go in and put her on the pot or whatever it was she wanted this time. I didn't mind. I hadn't come all this way to empty potties. They'd hired me as a housekeeper, and if the old woman was going to claw and spit every time I entered the room, well soon she would be dead and I'd still be a housekeeper.

They gave me a little room on the third floor, very hot in the hot season, but it had a basin in it, and a lovely view of the racecourse. Every Saturday afternoon, I would watch the races from that window, the natives swarming in through their entrance, and the rickshaws, and then the Europeans in their hats, with their motorcars and drivers waiting. After a while, I even knew which horse was coming in, although I could only see the far stretch. But I never went down myself, even though Saturday was my day off, and I never laid a bet.

I kept my money in a purse around my neck, day and night. I didn't trust the natives, and I didn't trust the old man I worked for. Every week, he counted out the shillings into my palm, and one before the last he would always look up into my face with a smile to see if I knew he had stopped too soon. The daughter told me it was a little game he played. But I never saw him play it on the natives. There were two of them, male and female, and they lived in a corrugated iron shack in the garden. My job was to tell them what to do, and to see they didn't mix up dishes for fish and dishes for meat, which they did all the time regardless.

It was the daughter who had recited the rules of the kitchen for me, delivering the whole palaver in that voice of hers, oh

Lord! And once, when there was butter left on the table and the meat was being carved, it was she who called me in and held out the butter dish as if it had bitten her on the nose. And the old man, with his serviette tucked into his collar, set down the carving knife and put a hand on her arm, and said, Sarah. So Sarah shut up.

There were other children, too, but they were grown up and married. Some of the grandchildren were older than this Sarah, older than me too. One of the grandsons fancied me. He was about my age, taller than the rest, and he had blue eyes and a lovely smile. But I hadn't come all the way out to South Africa to give pleasure to a Jewboy, even a charmer. I meant to make a marriage of my own, with a house and a servant, too.

And then, one day, the old man sent up a mirror for my room, and I stood it across one corner. It was tall and oval, and fixed to a frame so that I could change the angle of it by a screw on either side. And for the first time ever I could look at myself all at once, and there I was, tall and beautiful, and there I took to standing on a Saturday afternoon, naked in the heat, shameless before myself and the Lord.

Perhaps the old man knew. When I came into the room now, he would look up from his newspaper and smile at me if Sarah wasn't there. And under his gaze, it was as if we were switched around, he and I, and he were the mirror somehow, and I were he looking at myself and knowing what there was to see, the arms and the legs, the breasts and the thighs, the hair between them. And in this way I became a hopeless wanton through the old man's eyes, in love with myself and the look of myself. I couldn't help it. I smiled back.

And then, one Saturday afternoon, he knocked at my door and I opened it, and in he came as if we had it all arranged, and he went straight over to the mirror and looked at me through it. I looked, too, a head taller than he was, bigger in bone, and not one bit ashamed to be naked.

The first thing he did was to examine the purse around my neck, which I always wore, even in front of the mirror. He fingered it and smiled, and looked up into my face. I thought he might try to open it and start up one of his games, but he didn't. He left it where it was and put his hands on my waist, ran them up to my breasts and put his face into the middle of them. And then he took them one at a time, and used his lips and his tongue and the edge of his teeth, and all this silently except for the jangle of my purse and the roar of the races outside. And, somehow, he unbuttoned himself and had his clothes off and folded on the chair without ever letting me go. And we were in and out of the mirror until he edged me to the bed and there we were, in the heat, under the sloping ceiling, the old man and me, me and me, and I never once thought of saying I wasn't that sort of girl. And when he had gone and I found a pound note on the table, I didn't think so then, either. Money was what there was between us. I was hired as a housekeeper. And he had given me my mirror.

She found out about it, of course, the old cow downstairs. I heard her coughing out her curses at him, whining and weeping. But he didn't say much. And when Sarah came to find me in the kitchen parlor and announced in that voice of hers that I was never to go into her mother's room again, who did she think she was punishing?

Still, I felt sorry for Sarah, ugly little thing, flat in the chest, with the thin arms and the yellow skin, and a little moustache on the upper lip. I would have told her how to bleach it, but she wouldn't look at me now. Nor would she look at her father. She sat at the table with her eyes fiercely on the food, saying nothing at all. It was only to her mother that she would speak willingly, rushing into the front parlor when she came home from school, performing her recitations there, as if the old woman could understand a word of them.

For me, the house was separated in another way—up there, where it was airy and he came to kneel before me in silence, and down here the dark sickness, the smells of their food and the sounds of their language, the natives mooching around underfoot.

And meanwhile, my money mounted up. The old man kept to the habit of leaving some for me every time. Not always a pound, but never less than two and six. After a while, there was far too much to fit into the purse, so I hid the notes in a place I had found between the mirror and the wooden backing of it, and the larger coins inside the stuffing of my pillow. And, one Wednesday, when I had the afternoon off, I took it out of the

Building Society

hiding places and went down to the Building Society and put it in there. But still I wore my purse around my neck, and he loved to notice it there, and to smile as he began to unbutton.

His teeth were brown from the pipe, with jagged edges to them, and his legs and arms were thin and yellow like Sarah's, with black hair curling. But I didn't have to ask myself what it was about his oldness and his ugliness that I waited for so impatiently at my mirror. The younger men, the beautiful young men I saw going to the races, or on my way into town, or even the sons and the grandsons of the household, who were always looking at me now, but not in the same playful way—they would bend me to themselves, these young men, require a certain sort of looking back at them, and a laughing into the future. Oh no.

In the evenings, I brought the old man his sherry on a tray. He drank a lot for a Jew—two or three sherries, and wine, too, when he felt like it. And then once he looked up at me as I put down the tray, and there I was in that moment wondering how I could bear to wait until Saturday, and somehow he knew this because that night he came up the back stairs after Sarah was quiet in her room, and in the candlelight it was even better, the curves and the colors, my foot in his hand, pink in the candlelight as he put it to his cheek, and then held it there as he slid his other hand along the inside of the thigh. And I have never felt so strongly the power of being alive.

And then one Saturday afternoon, I was at the mirror waiting, and the door opened and it was Sarah to say they had called in the doctor, her mother was dying. Except that she didn't get it out because of the sight of me there, naked, with my purse around my neck. And I just smiled at her, because this was my room and she had no business coming in without knocking, and also I liked the look on her face as she gazed at me. And then, as I sauntered to the wardrobe for something to cover myself with, she said, I knocked, but you didn't hear, and she said it so politely for once, and in a normal voice, that I turned and I saw that she was crying, the eyes wide open and staring while the tears found a course around the nose and into the mouth. And she looked so frail, gaping there like a little bird, and she would be so lost now that the cursing old bitch was actually dying, that I went to her, naked as I was, and put my arms around her, and she didn't jump back, but buried her face between my breasts just as her father did, and held me around the waist, snorted and wept against me for a while.

The races are on, I said, to calm her down, and, Shall I dress and come downstairs? But she just held on tighter, and I saw that she was looking at us in the mirror, and there we were, a strange pair hugged together, when he arrived in the doorway behind us, and even so we didn't turn, but stood there, all three of us staring at each other until he said something to her in their language and she sort of melted on the spot, folded down onto the floor in front of me, her hands around my ankles, weeping again. And of course I knew it had happened, the old woman was dead, and that it would change everything, had changed things already. There he stood in my mirror, a tired and ugly old man, muttering something to his youngest daughter. She would take over now, this strange bird at my feet. It was the way it would be, that I knew. And I must get dressed and find my way in the world.

Railway Hotel

2

AFTER THAT, THERE WAS NEVER A PLACE where I didn't have a mirror. It was fixed in me, this way of considering myself, I couldn't do without it. With the belly beginning to swell, I liked to notice the blue of the veins threading through the skin, and then the browns of the breasts, and the sag, the hips thickening bit by bit.

The old man settled me into the Railway Hotel and sent money every week in a packet with the native boy. I had to worry him a little to get him to keep it up——making mention of the authorities, or the man in the next-door room who worked on the morning paper. The old man understood. He'd not been in the country that long himself, and seemed always mindful of what could be taken away again. So he sent the money, and sometimes, after dark, arrived himself. And then we'd fall into it again, he and I, the child in me only increasing the terrible longing, so that I could hardly walk in the street any more for wanting any man who might pass by. Even the old Jew would do.

I wore a wedding ring, but nobody in the hotel was fooled, of course. They saw the old man sauntering in whenever he pleased. They watched me in the dining room, how I cut my meat and dabbed at my mouth with the serviette. If I looked up, they looked away. Sometimes I liked to catch them at it, staring down at my plate one minute and then looking up quickly as if I'd been asked a question. Only the newspaperman with the terrible rubbled skin would give me a smile, and I'd smile back. I've always gone in for that sort of skin on a man. There is a manliness to it, and it makes them shy.

Once, before I left England, I was sitting in a train, and a gentleman with that sort of skin himself was settled in opposite me, his lower half all wrapped in a blanket, the legs useless. The upper half of him, though, was beautifully normal, broad and strong, even the neck. As the train lurched out of the station, one leg slipped forward and he pulled it back, using all the might of his arms. And then he kept looking to see if I'd noticed, and so, to help things a little, I asked him whether it had been the War that had done it. And yes, he said, oh yes, the War. There were so many of them broken up by the War that I couldn't help blurting out that I was going out to South Africa to be a housekeeper quite soon, I was only waiting for my passage.

And then he turned to look out of the window. Oh, he said, quite softly, what a waste that is. Oh, what a waste.

But really it was he who was wasted, not I, except that I couldn't tell him so because there was no way back for him and I had a future all before me.

When he turned to me, he was red in the face and staring.

Would you make a fuss, he said, if I asked you one favor? I thought, then, he'd want to kiss me. Often they did. But no, that wasn't it. Would I lock the compartment door, said he, and unbutton my bodice, just to let him have a look? He would never ask my name, and he would never touch me.

I did what he asked. And then I untied the skirt and the petticoat, too, and let them fall to the floor. I wanted him to see everything that was going to waste, the whole of me. And I wanted to read my chances in his face. There it was—the skin turning purple and the tears in the eyes. Oh God, he whispered, oh God, God, God.

And then I'd had enough, and pulled the clothes back on. Just as well he was a gentleman, because now I knew how he could have used his skills to have me any way he wanted, never mind the way he was. And there I'd be now, married to a cripple, and making his tea, and him correcting the way I talk, the way I lay the table. And nothing gone to waste to his way of thinking.

❦

My room in the hotel was small, with a window looking out over the alleyway. There was a bed and a basin, and a wardrobe with mirrors on the insides of the doors. I could leave them open altogether, which I usually did, or stop them at an angle to take a look at the back of me, the bottom, rounded out beautifully as if nothing was going on on the other side.

Mrs. Poynton, the proprietress, was a widow, said she. Certainly, she had the look of a widow—sharp-nosed and out for herself in all things. With regard to me, the lips were pressed into a straight line, edge to edge. Here's the rent, Mrs. Poynton. Mmmm. Mrs. Poynton, the w.c. is running over again today. Mmmm. But there was always the smell of whiskey about her, and her Wednesday and Saturday afternoons were off to the races in the tram, and then back again with a face like a fiddle.

One day, coming in from the street, I passed a man going out of the hotel very fast, coat and hat and stick. And there, in the front parlor, was Mrs. Poynton heaving and gasping, holding a hanky to her mouth to stop the noise.

What's the trouble, Mrs. Poynton? I asked from the doorway. And, Can I be of some help?

She looked up then, the face even uglier with tears. Get out, you little trollop! she screamed. Get out of my sight!

But it had come to me all at once, coming in through the front door, that there was providence in that man rushing down the steps. It was as if he had been rushing out to let me in, as if I had been waiting all this time to be let in, and more than waiting even, heading towards what waited for me inside.

Mrs. Poynton, I said, if it's money you're in need of, perhaps I can be of some assistance?

She looked up then, the mouth open, for once. What? she said.

Across the road, a train had just come in. The din started up, with the rickshaws whistling and the porters yelling. I waited a bit for it to die down, and then I said again, If it's money you're after, I could find a way, perhaps.

What way? asked she in a small voice unbecoming to her.

I sat down in one of her bony little chairs. Who was that man? I asked.

He's from the bank, said she, meek as ever. She took a piece of paper from her lap and held it out to me. He has to have the money by Friday, she whispered.

I took the paper and looked at the sums written on it. But, with the old crow watching me, I couldn't work it out in my usual way. So I stood up and said, Let me see what can be done. And out I went as if I knew it all, up to my room.

There I spread the paper out on the bed and had a good look. It was quite easy, after all. So much owing by such and such a date, final notice of same. I got out a pad of paper and a pencil, wrote down the amount, divided it by twelve for the months, and then by four for the weeks, and then by five for the years to come. I tore off the page, folded it up, and put it into my pocket. Then I wrote a note to the old Jew, telling him to come to me that night. URGENT, I wrote bold enough for even him to understand. And down I went for an envelope to Mrs. Poynton, which she gave me as quickly as she could snatch it from the front hall desk. And, Do you need the boy to take it over for you? she asked.

And so off it went and over he came that night, all red in the face with agitation. I had barely let him into the room when he started up in that language of his, waving the note at me, pointing at it and saying, No! No! No! Perhaps Sarah had got hold of it first, probably she had. Well, if that was the case, too bad. I went for the bottle of sherry I kept in the wardrobe for his visits, to calm him down. But he would have none of that either, muttering and mumbling and carrying on. So there was nothing for it but to fetch the bank paper and show him the amount that was owing on the place.

He sat down then, and pushed up his little spectacles onto the bald forehead, frowned down at the paper. I waited, wondering how to get it across that he could be rid of the cost of me and of the child forever in this one lump sum. My own money I would not touch for the purpose, even if it had been enough, which it wasn't, by far. Every week, I put what was left after the rent into the purse around my neck. And every month I went to the Building Society and added it in there. But that money was mine in one way, and this I wanted in another.

Too much, he said, shaking his head. Then he laughed, all the brown teeth showing, and tried to hand the bank paper back. And that's when I made for the door, intending to go to my newspaperman to say the Lord only knew what—something, anyhow, that would take the smile off the old man's face. But I didn't make it to the door handle before he called me back, still laughing. And it was then that I drew the paper with my own calculations out of my pocket, and gave it to him, and leaned over his shoulder to show him how I had added it all up on the one side, and then divided and divided again on the other, five years of payments and that would be that. And somehow I managed, after all, to get it across that I wanted his use of me paid up all at once, and I wanted it before Friday, and I wanted it in cash.

And then, before he could look down again at the balance owing, I settled onto his lap and took the spectacles off the head, giving him to understand that he wouldn't be losing me into the bargain, which wasn't the case at all, because, for the first time ever, I was with him only for the money, and even as he laid down the bank paper with a sigh, and pushed me gently to my feet, got up himself and led me in front of the mirrors—even as he unbuttoned me and undid me there, and then kneeled down at my feet as usual, the bald head smooth and round as my belly, and the warmth starting up in my thighs—even then there was a haste in me to have it over with, and a need, for once, to cry.

Railway station

3

AND THEN, BY SATURDAY, I, AGNES LA
G r a n g e, was the new proprietress of the Railway Hotel, and
Mrs. Poynton was packing, still in some surprise. Perhaps the
whiskey had got in the way of her common sense, but somehow
she'd had it in mind that I would be glad to hand over the old
Jew's money and she'd go on just as before, and so would I,
except that she'd owe the money to him instead of the bank, and
maybe she'd say good morning to me once in a while. Well, now
she was packing and I had left instructions with the Indian
waiter that the old man was to be stopped at the door with
excuses.

Anyway, my time was coming on. I could feel the child wanting to be out, and myself getting ready for the moment. I took the
large corner room right off the upstairs verandah for myself.
Mrs. Poynton's little flat behind the parlor was too far from the
life of the street for my liking, and too dark. Anyway, with a
cleaning out and a painting up, the rooms down there would
fetch more together than the one I was taking. And there'd be a
little room left over for a breakfast room, too.

The man at the bank had been surprised that I wanted to

hand over all the money rather than leave some for myself and some still owing to him. Every now and then, he took a glance down at the belly, as if I might have forgotten what lay in store for me. But I had a fair idea how he made his money and I knew how I had come by mine. No, I said, this is the way I wish it to be. And when he asked what name I would like on the deed, and Mrs. Poynton looked up as if she'd just sat on a needle, I smiled, because I had already been across the road to the City Hall, where I'd paid out almost all the money in my purse to have the new name recorded. Agnes La Grange. It was a lovely thing to spend the money on, because The Grange was where I'd been born, and where I would have died, with nothing to my name but a life of service had I not taken it into my head to better myself. And the "La" had come to me by chance because there it was on a banner at the front entrance of the City Hall—"La Bohème."

❧

The newspaperman was the only one who didn't come up to me now with stories about Mrs. Poynton this and Mrs. Poynton that, and how glad they were, and so forth. Not he. He just gave me his shy smile, trying to keep his eyes from my stomach. And when the child was born at last, and the doctor went away, it was he who knocked first at my door, and came in with a bunch of daisies.

He went straight to the crib and peered in so intently that it was as if he were the father and looking for himself in the face. But there was nothing of him in the child and very little of me either. There she was, opening and closing the little fists, with those dark eyes and a head of black curls. And for all the babies I'd seen my mother bring into the world, I couldn't believe that this one, different from them in all the details, was my own. And I said, I can't think what to call her. And that's when he said, Oh, why don't you call her Allegra?

He was all blotched red with blushing. And so I suggested some sherry, and told him where to fetch it from the wardrobe, and to put the daisies in the basin if he would. And there we sat, he and I, drinking to Allegra La Grange, and the sherry making everything seem lovely for a while, and him going into a whole palaver about a poet who'd been the father of Allegra, and so forth, until the baby started up with a shriek, and that got on my nerves immediately.

I might have known I would not be a natural mother. The whole thing felt like another form of service. It was one thing to find the right name for the baby, and to look into the crib and wonder about life, but it was quite another to know that that shriek would be following me about, whatever I did, until the day I died. Downstairs, the natives would be taking advantage of my confinement, the waiters too. I had threatened them, put one in charge of the other, but it would make no difference in the end. Without me to watch them, they'd be running off with the sugar and the silver and Lord knows what else. The only one I trusted in the place was this newspaperman, and he was gone morning to night, every day of the week.

And suddenly there were tears rolling down my cheeks. Not that I was entirely miserable, but that he was there to see them, I suppose. The fact is, I felt sorry for myself and pleased with myself all at once. And that's when he reached for my hand and said, You're very young to be taking on all this, you know, which made me weep some more, and then the shrieking only got louder, and I asked him please to bring me the baby, and if he wouldn't mind staying to talk a bit more, I'd like that, too. And so he sat on the easy chair, angled away from me, with the ears bright red at the thought of what was going on behind him, although he might have taken a look any hour of the day at the native girls sitting along the pavement, with their beautiful brown breasts, and their beads, and their babies good as gold.

And meanwhile the child screamed on and refused to feed, and my breasts were swollen like rocks. I tried to think what my mother had done, but all I could remember was a baby at the breast and the knitting and sewing she went on with regardless, the orders she gave me, too. And I wondered how women the world over, natives included, went in for this sort of thing time after time.

He was saying over his shoulder that there were things to do in the town if one wanted to get out, plays and recitals and so forth. Perhaps I'd thought of a nanny for the baby, when I was ready to get up?

I'm ready to get up now, said I, tying the nightie closed because the child had fallen asleep after all that. How can I run this place from a bed? You can turn around now.

He was older than he looked, and he crossed his legs, thigh over thigh, like a gentleman. But there was lacking in him a sort of manly need that came and took what it wanted regardless, even the old Jew had that. And maybe, I thought, this is what it means to be a gentleman, all the blushing and so forth, and maybe even the gentleman on the train would have been different if I'd been a proprietress then.

And I was beginning to wonder how it would be with a husband of my own, and a house and servants too if the longing stopped, when suddenly, there was some sort of commotion going on downstairs, the Indian waiter's voice rising into a screech, doors opening and a clattering up the stairs. Out went the newspaperman to see what the matter was, and the next thing, there was the old Jew storming into the room, red in the face himself, and the Indian waiter behind him shouting, Madam! Madam! Here he is coming! and me sitting there like the Queen of Sheba while the old man stopped dead in front of the crib, and behind him all the rest, even the servants gathered at the door, their hands over their mouths.

He stared into the crib, where she was sleeping now like a small, dark angel. He reached down to touch the hair and the little face, and his spectacles misted up so that he had to take them off and give them a wipe. And then he started up some sort of winding chant, the voice breaking here and there, and it struck me that he didn't even know if it was a girl or a boy, so I pointed and said, Girl, girl. And he looked at me softly and said, Leah. *Lay-a*. And I said, my eyes on the newspaperman, Her name is Allegra, but she will have yours in the middle. Allegra Leah La Grange. And I knew it was the old cow's name I was saddling her with, and myself who would have the burden of it, but there was nothing I could do. Leah was her real name just as Agnes was mine. And if she came to hate me, this child, the way the old woman had hated me, well there was nothing I could do about that either. Agnes and Leah. That was the way it would be from now on.

4

WELL, I MADE A MARRIAGE WITH THE newspaperman after all. Part of it was due to the child, who loved him from the start, settling into his arms and looking up into that face as if he were the Mother of God. And part because he loved me with a great tenderness, everything about me, steadying the rage that had come out lately in me like the devil itself. It could start with almost nothing at all—a tablecloth stained, a fork in the wrong place—and then towering up it would go, while the poor old native stood there, hanging his head in silence.

And what was it about? A tablecloth? A fork? Not likely. It was more to do with the luck I had come into and the life it brought with it. Up there, in the old Jew's attic, I had had myself to know and my future to be sure of. But here was the future now, and the life was out of it somehow. Of course, as the newspaperman said, I was very young for all this. Still, if I looked at it his way, I could see too well how things would go along and along from here. And, when he would start up on Allegra this and Allegra that, and where we would send her to school and so forth, then the rage would settle right deep in the stomach like a growl.

We put her in the little room next to ours, and had a door built between them. If there was getting up to do in the night, it was he who did it. And then, as soon as she could climb out of the cot, first thing in the morning there she was at his side of the bed, saying, Daddy, Daddy! And the more this went on, the more I was on the side of the old Jew. The child was his, with the eyes and the nose, and the wiry little body and blue-black hair. Just looking at her could take me back to that little room under the sloping ceiling, the races going on outside. And now here I was in a great, huge bed with a man who switched out the light every night, and then turned to me, and said, May I have a little kiss, or are you tired?

Well, yes, I was tired, I was always tired with the lights out and that voice in my ear. It wasn't as if I hadn't tried to have things different. Once, on my birthday, after a bottle of Champagne, I brought up the idea of a mirror and what could take place before it. But what was the point? By the time I got him upstairs and standing there, he was asking me what he should do next and to tell him quietly so as not to wake up Allegra. And it seemed gone forever then, that way of being alive. And I began to cry with the misery of it, the Champagne helping things along. And then there he was again, wanting to know what the matter was, I only needed to tell him. But, of course, I couldn't tell him, what would have been the point?

From the first, I had guessed how it would be with him, and now that it was that way, who could I blame but myself?

Meanwhile, the hotel was getting on nicely, making a steady profit from the traveling salesmen who came in by train, and also residents like the newspaperman, who couldn't afford much but had pride enough to pay on time. I knew what a pot of paint could do to cheer a place up, so I had the dark old wallpaper painted over in cream, the woodwork, too. And on a Saturday night, we had dancing now in the dining room, with the double doors opened to the parlor and a small band playing in one corner.

I hired a new cook, too, who could do more than boiled fish and white sauce. I did the marketing myself, so I knew what came in. Every Monday, the cook and I made up the menus together. And if there was anything missing, it was his wages that suffered.

All this was good, and there were very few complaints. But still, when I passed a mirror now, or a window, and I saw myself in it, there was no longer a lifting of the heart, but rather a sort of sadness, and sometimes a panic, and often a rage. Because there I was, still beautiful, and there at my skirt was Leah, looking up at me with those great dark eyes of hers. And I didn't want to go back, and I couldn't go back, but I wanted to go on in a different way.

The newspaperman suggested another child right off, as soon as we married. When I said no, he said we could wait. And when I said never, he just smiled as if he knew better. And so I went to the doctor and told him I wanted the whole matter taken care of from now on and forever. And he said, oh no, the husband must be consulted for this sort of thing. And then I found the name of another doctor, right down at the docks, where they do anything for a price. But even he told me the things that could happen, the things that had happened to others.

You are very young, said he, and, What if you move on one day and find a man whose child you may want to bear?

And as he was saying those words, I felt such hope again for the future that my throat closed tight with tears. So I watched and I listened when he took out a chart and explained how to count this way and that way from the middle of the month, and what to do regardless.

But still, I was thinking to myself that not wanting a man might be what made it easier not to have his child. And that if the old Jew walked in of an afternoon—which he had never once done, not since the day she was named—there would be the danger, even now. We would be up in the room and locking the doors, standing there before the mirror again with the light coming in through the curtains. Nor would it be any different with a sailor or a soldier or the king of the castle. It was the law of nature and the will of the Lord. And who was I to understand it better than that?

When I came out of the doctor's building, I went for a walk

The tram to the docks

along the docks, looking at the ships and the water. There were sailors everywhere, of course, and taverns, and Coloured girls laughing and offering themselves at a price. Oh, there was life there, and I loved everything about it, even the sour stench of the whaling station at the Bluff, and the whales themselves, all mottled and floating like balloons.

The sailors whistled and carried on, of course, but the Coloured girls didn't like it at all, shouting at me to go back where I came from, with their rotten teeth and language. But I just walked on, happy. It was easy to get down here on the tram, I would come whenever I wished for a taste of life. Even now, there were three sailors dogging my steps, clueless young men jabbering in a foreign language. They didn't know, these young fools, that you can't go after a woman in a pack. I would have had any one of them right there behind a tea crate, forgetting completely about what the doctor had just told me, so powerful was the return of my hope. But, with the three of them behind me, I had to keep my eyes to the front, a lady with a hat and a handbag.

5

ONE AFTERNOON I MADE A FRIEND DOWN
there. She sat on a bench, looking out at the bay, and of course
the sailors were at it, hanging over the railings of the ships and
making remarks. She was not at all one of the street girls, but
pale and plainly dressed in a dark skirt and white blouse, the
thin brown hair screwed into a bun. I sat down next to her and
had just begun saying, Oh, isn't it lovely down here? when
she nearly jumped out of her skin, so far was she into another
world. And that world, as she told me when we got talking,
was the one she'd left on the ship. And now here she was,
come out from England to marry one man, and in love with
another, who had gone on in the *Empress of India*, up the coast
to Beira.

It was a lovely story. The man she loved was a hunter, and
the one she was to marry was a doctor. She herself was a nurse,
with the date set for the wedding, and the reception to be held
at the Majestic. But in six months or so, the *Empress of India*
would be back, with the hunter on it.

I don't know why I'm telling you all this, said she with a
hopeless sort of smile. And then, Yes, I do know why.

But she didn't ask for my advice, and so I didn't give it. She was not like me, this Constance. For her it was one man or another, never herself for the future. And so I told her how I had come out as a housekeeper, and that I had the Railway Hotel now, and the child, and the newspaperman as a husband. And still I was restless.

She took a good look at me then, and said, But what shall I do? And what could I tell her? Go on after that hunter and find out how it is to be left behind and grow bitter waiting all your life for a man? Or, learn to put up with the one you have found, and leave that hunter in your heart to grow old with?

And when she asked again, But what would *you* do? I said, without a thought, I would marry neither. And she hung her head then, because she had hoped I would have gone after the hunter so that she could have thought, It's all very well for her. But it wasn't all very well for me, and I told her this, although in a vague sort of way. She looked up then, and listened carefully. And, somehow, telling her my story was unraveling that hard knot of rage in my stomach, because I thought, I'll find my own way, regardless, it's how I was before and how I'll always be. And I was very glad to have a friend, and invited her to the hotel for tea the next day.

She was staying at the Majestic, around the corner. The doctor had found a flat on the ridge for after the wedding. There was furniture to be bought, a suite of this and a suite of that, and she had no heart for the purpose. So I said I'd help her if she liked, we could go together, but first she had to decide what she was going to do. I knew already, of course, and so did she, that she would marry the doctor, it was only a matter of hardening herself up for the purpose. But we took some time talking it over, and I said the hunter could always send his letters care of me, which seemed to cheer her up no end.

So away we went, under the whistles of the sailors, to catch the tram together.

❧

When she came for tea, I found out that her doctor was the first one I had gone to. And even though I remembered little about him except the spindly fingers and the small, pale eyes, I felt more sorry for her than before. Still, she herself seemed quite cheered up, with a bit of color in her cheeks now, and there was even talk of how to hire a servant. And then Leah was brought in by the nanny, and Constance admired the child enormously, stroking the thick, black curls and inviting her onto her lap. And I could see she was thinking that one of her own might change things around for her entirely.

Seeing Leah sitting there, opening her little beak for a sugar cube, I felt proud that she was mine. And when Constance asked her name, and the child said straight out, Leah, I laughed and clapped my hands. And so the child laughed and clapped hers too. She was Leah. And only the newspaperman used the name that he himself had given her.

Every day, every week, he seemed to love the child more, and while she loved him back, and let him teach her her letters and her numbers, spelling things out and adding them up before she was even out of nappies, it was myself she was always on the lookout for. And soon I was taking the long way round to my room so that I wouldn't have to go through all that running up, and Mummy! Mummy!, and the jumping on the lap, and begging for a sweet. It made me tired, this sort of thing, when I wasn't really tired at all.

If anything woke me up in the night now, it was the thought that I was bound to the newspaperman for the child's sake. But then I would get up and go to look at her as she slept, and oh, there she was, the little fingers wrapped around the satin edging of the blanket. And I would touch them, and the dark curls on the pillow, the cheek flushed with sleep. And no, she wasn't his at all. She was hardly even mine. And I was bound to no man, not even to her father.

Agnes, said Constance, would you consider being my matron of honor? And is the little one old enough to be flower girl?

So it was done. The hunter was shut up into her heart, and there was I, conspiring with her about lace and lilies and petticoats. And I wondered how long it would be after the wedding until she was here, asking for his letters, tearing them open and reading them standing up, and again sitting down. And then there'd be nothing for a while until down he came himself from the interior, all bearded and brown, and by then she'd be large with the doctor's child. In she'd waddle, choosing a straight-backed chair for the backache, and he would take one look and be into his whiskey. And on she'd go for the rest of her life thinking she'd had a narrow escape, and that, somehow, she had me to thank for it. But there was nothing narrow about it. It was as wide as the sea for people like her. And I liked her the better for the way she was.

⁊

The wedding was a grand affair, first the church, and then the main hall of the Majestic, all done up with ribbons and lilies, and a whole orchestra playing on the dais. I'd made my own dress in a hurry, and Leah's too, with the material and lace that Constance had brought out on the ship from England. Mine was plain, as she wished it to be, with beads along the hem, and room for improvement later. But Leah's was all flounced and fancy, with little satin ballet shoes, and a satin ribbon for her hair. I put rouge on the cheeks, which made her look less worried, although she could not stay behind me, but would insist on being there at my side down the aisle, holding on to the train too.

The newspaperman bought himself a tuxedo for the affair, but not until he had weighed up the uses of it against the cost, and then the cost against other things the money might be needed for. He also borrowed a camera from the office to take a picture of Leah and me all dressed up, and stood us at the entrance to the hotel, setting up the camera on the pavement. And there was something, for once, about the way he knew just what he was doing that made me glad he was my husband. And for a long time after, I remembered the sight of him there in that tuxedo, telling us to stand quite still, and then bending to take a look, the large hands gentle on the levers.

And when I danced with him at the reception, he seemed to know I'd softened towards him, because he took charge of the floor, sweeping me around it, dipping and changing directions. And people clapped, and Leah ran in, wanting him to pick her up, too. And so he did, but then he called over the nanny to take her to the hotel and put her to bed. And back we were, dancing every dance until the end. And all the while, there, at the edge of the dance floor, was a man with a cigar, who never took his eyes off me. They were bold eyes, as if he knew all about me start to finish, not in the way of the old Jew, but in the way of a man who has had all the women in the world and will go on having them, and knows what he sees when he sees it. And then the newspaperman saw him, too, and bent over to whisper to me that he was on the City Council and owned half the town, and had I seen the way I'd caught his eye?

And when I went off to the powder room, there was the tycoon waiting for me when I came out. I bow before beauty, Madam, said he. And, although I was not taken in by this sort of performance, there was a steely charm in him. Before I knew it, his card was in my hand, and he said, Don't let me wait too long. And that was a little better, because he was looking at my eyes for an answer, and, still looking, he touched the inside of my arm above the elbow. And I thought, Oh no, I won't be one out of many for you, Sir. But I said, I think you're too used to having your own way, Sir. And I smiled as I said it, and tucked his card into my bodice. And then back I went to the dance floor.

6

As it turned out, he couldn't bear the wait, because there, one afternoon, was the smell of his cigar floating up the front stairs, and the Indian waiter after it, sent to call me down. By the time I arrived, the tycoon had settled himself onto the couch in the parlor and held his watch in his hand with a frown.

Well, Sir, said I, so here you are. And there indeed he was, slipping the watch back into the pocket, and inviting me to sit down, too. But I don't sit in my own parlor at the invitation of a stranger, even one who owns half the town. So I took up a position beside the old wing chair, with my arm resting over the back of it. Would you like a cup of tea? I asked.

He folded his arms and looked about a bit as if he'd never been in such a place before and couldn't trust the tea. And then, suddenly, there was the steely smile again and his eyes straight on my own. Had I ever considered expanding my talents to somewhere up on the ridge, he wanted to know? A place with a view of sea? And was I aware that the old Avondale Hotel up there was on hard times and would sell out at a price?

The Avondale. I'd seen pictures of it, with its green verandah and white pillars and the lawns overlooking the bay.

But I could never pay the price, said I, softening at the knees and sitting down after all.

He took a draw on the cigar then. Listen to me, he said. In another ten years, this place will be taken over by the Municipal Corporation for less than the price you paid for it. They'll tear it down to widen the road to the Esplanade, it's all in the plans. What is it, anyway, but a glorified boardinghouse? Look to the future, my girl.

He had an amazing power, this man who owned half the town, to give me a future of his own making, and then to cripple the one I had already. I picked up the bell and rang for tea after all, but when the waiter came in, the tycoon dismissed him and told him to close the door behind him.

He leaned forward, with the elbows on the knees. I'm always looking for a good investment, he informed me.

Then why don't you buy it yourself?

The smile again, as if I didn't know. He would own me along with half the town if he had his way. A hotel needs a strong hand to run it, is how he put the matter.

And although I was becoming more certain every minute that I should go nowhere with this man, least of all into debt, I could not take my mind from that view of the sea from up there, and even Leah running about in such a place. And, in a manner of thinking, I was there already and trying to take myself

Indian waiters

back, because a great greed had got hold of me, and I wrestled with it like the man with the python in the circus. And all the while the tycoon watched.

He pulled out a little notebook from his jacket, and unscrewed a pen, and began to jot things down. When he was finished, he looked up. Come and sit over here next to me, said he. And so I did. And there, in neat, perfect numbers, was the amount I had paid for the Railway Hotel, and then what they would take for the Avondale. The one minus the other was a sum exactly twice what the old Jew had given me.

And who will supply the difference? I asked, my heart beating so high in my throat that I had to swallow in the middle.

He laid one hand over mine, cool and dry. That, my dear, you can leave to me.

But, mad as I was to have that place for myself, I had never left anything up to anyone in my life. Oh no, said I, I need to know everything before I can agree. I must take a real look at the hotel too. I've only seen the pictures in the paper.

My motorcar and driver's waiting outside, said he, standing up.

And so, in twenty minutes, there I was, walking in through the great doors with him, and there were the Indian waiters in turbans and sashes, and a lovely breeze on the front verandah, and the smell of grass and scones and ladies' perfume. Upstairs there was a whole suite that he had to himself whenever he wanted it, and Champagne waiting in a silver bucket, although

I hadn't heard him ask. And when I went to the window, there was the sea, all silver too, with a haze across the horizon, and a ship leaving the harbor. And then he came up behind me, put his hands around my waist and his chin on my shoulder.

But it was the place, not the man, that I wanted, and I said I might prefer tea to Champagne. And I'd like to see where I'd be living too. And also there were things to consider—a school for the child, for instance, and my husband's wishes, too. And not even this did it, he just moved his hands up to my bosoms and bent to kiss my neck.

So I pulled myself away and went to sit in a chair. He smoothed down his hair and sat, too. And I was pleased to see that he was still smiling, because, fool that I was, I wanted the place despite him. But you can't have anything despite such a man and he knew it. So he phoned down for some tea. I might have known then, even in the way he didn't watch me pour, that there was nothing of myself to increase with this man or of him to increase in me. It was as much a question of winning as of wanting, for him. And if someone here were to win and someone to lose, I had an idea of which I would be.

Still, I let him show me how it could be done, my quarter of the money to his three-quarters, and a thirty percent share of the place for me because I would have the running of it and certain other responsibilities, too. The offer, said he, would be drawn up before the end of the week, and the contracts, too, if it came to that. He himself would have the place looked over for

Avondale

white ants and borer. And perhaps I'd like his help in doing something about my wardrobe in the meantime?

My wardrobe? As soon as he dropped me back at the Railway Hotel, I went straight up to the room and looked in the mirrors, front and back. I took the dresses out one by one and held them up to me. I was clever with a needle and I liked a bit of a frill here and there, but who would quarrel with that?

I called down to the waiter to bring me up the English magazines from the parlor table, and laid them out on the bed, and looked into them carefully. And when the newspaperman came in, I asked his opinion, too, even though I might have known he'd be useless. If the tycoon noticed everything and watched nothing in me, then this man was neither a noticer nor a watcher. He had loved me first as a fallen woman, and then as a mother and now as a wife. And when I told him what had happened that afternoon, and about the Avondale being up for sale, and the tycoon from the wedding coming over without asking, and what he had proposed, well the stupid man could only gape in wonder at the prize he'd won for himself. And never once did he ask me whether the tycoon was after anything but buying up the Avondale.

7

ONE MORNING'S SHOPPING WITH THE tycoon was all it took. There he sat in the armchair, and me next to him, while the saleslady at Grenville's brought out the dresses one by one. And then he'd choose this or that, and she'd have a model put it on, and find a hat to match, and gloves, too. And then he'd either nod or shake his head, and if he nodded, she hung the dress on a rail, and then out she went to fetch the next one.

It didn't matter what I liked, he paid no attention at all, even waved a hand to shut me up. And when it was time, finally, for me to try on what he'd chosen, and I suggested that all these ecrus and pale mauves and whites piped in navy blue were not to my liking, well he winked at the saleslady, and she gave a little smirk. And I knew right then I'd never feel the same again in my old clothes and colors.

And so out I came with the dresses, and the jackets and hats to match, and shoes and gloves as well. And if I felt strange for a while, then soon I became used to this new plain way of looking. People noticed me differently, too. Even the Coloured girls at the docks stopped carrying on every time I went down there. And in a way it was lonelier, this new style of looking he had given me. And in a way I was proud.

When Leah saw my old dresses all piled up on the bed, she went mad with desire to put them on herself. And so I dressed her up in them, and opened the wardrobe doors for her to see herself. And, for once, she laughed out loud with happiness, pulled one off to put another on, hats too, and mittens, and shoes. I said I would shorten them, and take them in to fit her, but she wouldn't have it, she wanted them just as they were, flapping and trailing around her and smelling of my perfume. She carried them off, one by one, to her room, and there she kept them in a trunk that I had given her, and even when we moved up to the Avondale, the trunk was the first thing she wanted put on the lorry.

The contract had taken longer than the tycoon had thought, but it was done, of course, and the Railway Hotel bought for exactly the sum he had named. Just who had bought it took me a while to work out, because it wasn't a person but a Pty. Ltd., and when I found out that he himself was the owner of that Pty. Ltd., he gave me a whole palaver about the world of business, and the need to own certain enterprises for reasons of taxation. And even though I wasn't taken in by all this, and knew he had his reasons, I also knew I had my thirty percent up here on the ridge and a small salary to put in the Building Society every month, not to mention a suite of rooms all to myself, and a whole staff to get under the whip again.

He advised me to listen to the way the guests spoke, and to the words they chose, too. I should also learn to play croquet and tennis, said he, and to work out for myself to whom I should lose, and whom I should beat by how much. But I was never one for games, not caring whether I lost or won at them. And as for the way I spoke, the words and the voice were not for throwing into an old trunk like the frills and colors of my past, oh no. Still, I would go to sit under the thatch of the clubhouse and watch the tennis there, with Leah trailing after me down the grassy slope, draped like a queen in my old clothes, with a feathered hat on askew.

He had no time for children, this tycoon, and was bent on advising me to keep Leah out of the main rooms of the hotel. But in this matter, I ignored him. When she came in, everyone looked up with a smile, even the scowly old English Lord with his newspaper. She was never a child to make a noise, nor would she whine or cry in the company of strangers. She was hardly a child at all, except that she looked the part, with those great black eyes and those curls, and the lovely little voice she had for singing.

As soon as someone sat down at the piano, there she was, cocking her head like a little bird. And then, in our rooms, she would come out with the melody, perfect in every note. And so I taught her the songs I knew, in my own silly voice, *So we'll go no more a-roving*, and *When a laddie meets a lassie*, and she would have the tune first, and then the words, singing the song all over the place. It was a lovely thing in a child, this talent, and not a moment of shyness about it. If someone asked her to sing, or even put her up on the stage, where the orchestra played on a Saturday night, well she would link her hands together in front of her, the way I had taught her to, and out of the mouth would come the song, pure and beautiful.

It was Constance who suggested that the child should have singing lessons one day, because the voice was a thing that needed training, said she, before bad habits set in. Constance had a passion against bad habits, particularly in women, which she told me several times because I had taken up smoking myself. There was also the matter of the tycoon, said she. He was the doctor's friend, and had an eye for the women, even though he had a wife and children of his own. And when I laughed and told her that this I had known from the day of her wedding, she blushed, remembering her hunter, I suppose, who had neither written nor arrived himself, although six months was nearly up. I told her to watch out, one day soon he'd be pitching up out of nowhere, and she laughed, looking around the verandah to see if anyone could have overheard.

But still, Agnes, she whispered, watch out yourself.

And so I told her how the tycoon had had it all planned for us from the start, with the Champagne in a silver bucket, and how he'd bought me the clothes, and tried to change the way I spoke. And that even though I didn't trust him, we'd become partners, he and I. I could tell him things and ask him things, not like a mistress whining for attention, but as the proprietress of the Avondale Hotel. And as far as I was concerned, he could convince himself any way he pleased that it was he who had stopped the thing before it had started, because I had what I wanted for the moment, even though it still lacked a man to love.

And then she said, One could come along any day and turn it all upside down for you, you know. And I laughed again, because she was the one who had been turned upside down, and now here she was, right side up, laying down the law herself.

I preferred her to come to the hotel than to go myself to her flat, which depressed my spirits with its smell of Dettol and furniture polish and onions frying in the kitchen. Sometimes, she invited us for a dinner, and over we had to go. And then the doctor would ask the newspaperman what he thought should be done about the Colour Bar or the gold standard, sitting and puffing on his pipe like a teacher giving an exam. But it was the newspaperman who was the one to be giving exams, he'd gone to Oxford, although he never boasted.

And meanwhile Constance and I would sit on the couch, and she'd crochet her antimacassars while we talked about the servants. And then the telephone would ring, and out would go the doctor with his black leather grip, and the three of us were left to ourselves for coffee. And so I came to thinking that I should have told her to choose that hunter after all, because, even though he would have made her miserable, he would have kept the heart alive. Whereas this way, there would never be a time in her life again like the one she'd had on the ship, and how could she bear the thought of that?

For her part, she took to making up for my poor education with a trip to the library every week. It was for the sake of Leah, said she, and because knowledge is a wonderful thing, you find out about life, and also I would know what the guests were talking about if I needed to.

But Leah had the newspaperman to teach her, said I, and the guests talked only of themselves. Still, I read the books she chose for me, every week something new. And I found out all about Florence Nightingale and Robinson Crusoe, and what had happened to Rome in the end. And it seemed to me that the world hadn't changed much since the beginning of time, and whatever the Lord had in store for us, it was here on earth we must make our own way regardless.

And that's when she laughed, and called me a heretic, and suggested I come with her to church on a Sunday. But at this I drew the line. It was a long way I'd come from being frightened half out of my wits by the men of God, and I wasn't going back now.

8

AND THEN ONE DAY, ON MY WAY TO THE docks, I passed the Railway Hotel and saw a sign in the window. So I got off the tram to have a look. It said, "Private Hotel: Residents Only." The front door had a little window cut into it, and it was locked. When I rang the bell, the little window opened, and an Indian said, Yes? And so I told him who I was, and why I had come, and he just shut it again, leaving me standing there, with a scurrying going on inside, and some voices raised. And then at last he came back and opened the little window and said, Oh Madam, you cannot be coming in this place any more, Madam. And though I could hardly see around him, it was enough to work out what the hotel had become.

And so on I went, down to the docks. And there was the *Empress of India* just arrived, all white and beautiful with its smokestacks and portholes, and people coming down the gangway, and the natives stacking the luggage along the railway tracks. I stood on the dock as I had stood when first I arrived, watching the ladies and gentlemen calling to the porters, and the natives shouting to each other, and the smell of the whales, and the sun shining bright and cheerful in the middle of July.

And who would question me now if I stood with them myself, those ladies and gentlemen? And who would stop me if I went on board? And so up I went onto the gangway, and up onto the ship. And inside it was like England all over again, with the polished wood and the European waiters, and the closed-in smell of a dark place.

I was standing around in the lounge, wondering how to get up on the deck for some fresh air, when a man came over to me, all brown and bearded in his khaki togs.

May I be of assistance, Madam? said he, not bothering with a smile. There was a sharp look in the blue eyes and a stillness to him as he waited for an answer, and also a touchiness in the distance he kept between us. And I knew as surely as I knew anything that he was Constance's hunter.

How long does the boat stop here? I asked.

Three days, said he, giving me his arm.

Up on the deck, he found two chairs looking out over the bay. I told him I used to love coming down to the docks when I owned the Railway Hotel, and now it was turned into a brothel and I was at the Avondale, miles up on the ridge, with a view of the sea and the bay. And although I should feel rewarded, I felt punished or warned, I couldn't work out which. And he said nor could he when luck carried him along too fast. He was a hunter himself, said he, and luck always put him on his guard.

And oh how lovely it was for once to find a man without all the answers, and to be sitting there, looking out at the Bluff, and the sea wind blowing, and him helping me on with my cardigan, asking whether I'd like to come back to the ship tomorrow.

And of course I said I would, but I wished he'd asked me to stay right then, because I couldn't bear the thought of what might happen to get in the way of my coming back tomorrow, and of what could come along to carry him away himself. And at the same time it was as if the three days were gone already, and me left behind like Constance, or like those women in the books she gave me to read, watching their men go off to die in battle, and him not a real man at all, but just an idea of a man, nor me a real woman either.

And only then did I stop on the stairs on the way back down, and tell him that I knew who he was, and that Constance was my friend now, and providence must have brought me here, because otherwise he'd have been ringing on that bell at the Railway Hotel, asking for her by name through the little window.

Well, he smiled then, and said he'd known nothing of the Railway Hotel until now, she had only written to say she was marrying the doctor and that was that. And he stopped at the bend of the stairs and lifted my chin with one finger to stop the talk. And there was never a mention of Constance between us again.

Nor did anything come along to stop me going down to the

ship the next morning, or him waiting in the lounge, although I had not given him a time. He turned and went ahead when he saw me, leading me down some steps and along some corridors to his cabin. And even in there I might have known there would be no need for talking. He opened the little porthole window, and I went to look out, kneeling on the bunk, with the sun blinding on the water. When I turned back, there he was in the dark of the cabin, watching me in the mirror. And it was as if all the years I'd spent making my way with the wrong man were nothing, now that I was here, with him moving silently to take me in his arms, the raw smell of him and the fierce blue eyes. And I thought, If this man had horns and hooves it would only delight me more.

And then, lying back on the bunk, my head on his arm, I told myself what I would have told Constance, or anyone else for that matter—never ask about the future with such a man. But, no sooner was the thought in my head than I was asking, When do you think you'll be back, then? the voice cracking as I tried to make it jaunty.

I'm here now, said he, and I'll be back when I can.

And so, at last, I had fallen in love with a man, and quite impossibly, too. And, when Constance came for tea the next week, and said I looked a little pale, I gazed at her in wonder. How could she not see that I had caught the terrible sickness? The stupid sickness? That I was a stupid, doting woman, helpless and hopeless like any fool in a book, and where was the great future now?

9

AND SO ON IT WENT, MORE THAN FIVE years of it, either waiting for the man, or mourning when he went away. The present stretched endlessly into the future, and the future was measured by the six months until the ship arrived, and then by the six months more.

When he was gone, I wrote him letters. Lord, the letters! Twelve or twenty to his measly one. And how many times he read them, and whether he might have smiled at the things I told him I never knew. But, really, it wasn't to tell him things that I was writing, it was to comfort myself. Because while I was writing, there he was, with the blue eyes on me and the sly smile that I could draw out of him simply by saying the things I said. And then, when I'd finished a letter, it was as if he'd just gone away again, and so I would start another. And that's how the newspaperman came to find one of them, half written, and there he was with the page in his hand, very deep in silence, and the face purpled up with fury.

How long has this been going on? asked he, as if he had every right in the world to me and my desires. And, What sort of fool do you take me for?

Well, I answered both questions directly of course, and the whole hotel must have heard the flaming row. Everything came out of him all at once. I might have known, and, The sort of mother you've been, too. And that stung me at last, because I knew he was right. Right from the beginning, he'd been mother and father to the girl, and, if I loved her when I loved her, well it would never be enough.

In the books I read, there was nothing but joy in the hearts of the mothers, except when they weren't real mothers at all, but only stepmothers. And then it was all rage and fury, and the girls cowering under the rod or eating poisoned apples. But here was I, the real mother, and I thought, She'll not always be a child, and I'll not always be young and beautiful. And who will I have then but her? And who can I count on ever?

And so I wept, and Yes, said the newspaperman, you might well cry. You're selfish and you're primitive, and I hope he knows, whoever he is, what he's got hold of in you.

And when it was over, what did I do but write to the hunter to tell him about it, and especially the word *primitive*, which I knew would appeal to him because he used it about me himself, and not to condemn at all, but only in praise? And while I was about it, I told him I was considering a jaunt inland to see him, and what did he think about that?

Well, that night, the newspaperman didn't come to bed at all. And the next morning, I found he'd slept in the little study he had for himself, and ordered the staff to make up his bed on the divan from now on. So that was that with him.

As for the hotel, I'd find a spinster or a widow to run it for the month or two that I'd be gone. The tycoon wouldn't like it one bit, of course, but that was just too bad. He'd been looking very glum lately, which the newspaperman had put down to the state of things in the world these days, people losing all their money and jumping out of windows in America. Soon it would happen here, said he, it was only a matter of time.

All the more reason to go, I thought, and the sooner the better. And even though going might change everything around between the hunter and me, even though I knew in my heart that it would, well I wanted a change and I wanted a surprise after all these years. And so I sent a telegram to say I was coming, and please to meet the train. And the more I thought of it, the more thrilling the whole jaunt seemed to me. It would be like a story in one of Constance's books, and I didn't even know the ending.

But then, when the time actually came to leave, there was Leah watching the dresses going into the trunk one by one, and the mother-of-pearl hairbrush she still loved to play with. For five years now, she had been watching the mystery of my happiness and miseries, unconnected to her. And now there she was when the taxi pulled up, with her face against the glass of the front door, trying not to cry as the trunk and hatboxes went into the boot. And there I was, putting on a smile for her, wanting only a smile in return. But the tears came spilling down her cheeks at last, so that I ran back and hugged her, and began crying myself, saying, Darling, I'll be back as soon as I can, as if I had no choice but to go. And she hung on for dear life, sobbing into my neck, so that I had to unfasten each finger, and leave her standing there, turning her face from the guests going out for their afternoon walk.

And all the way down to the station I sobbed myself, and it was worse at the sight of anything to remind me of her, even the Railway Hotel. And I thought, Wherever you go and whatever you do now, there'll always be having to choose between what you want and what you're leaving behind.

10

It was a tiring journey, three days in the heat switching and changing and showing my papers for stamping. But it was lovely, too, stopping at the little towns, and then the plains of yellow grass and the umbrella trees, and the mountains blue in the distance. After a while, there were even animals to see—zebras and antelopes and giraffes with their babies, all looking up as we passed as if we were interrupting their tea. And every now and then the native children would come running from their kraals and dance next to the train, holding out their hands for sweets.

I had a coupé to myself all the way, and all the time in the world to think of where I was going, what I was leaving behind. And the funny thing was, now that I was going to see the hunter I wasn't at all sure I wanted him. And so, what was the point of the journey? To punish the newspaperman for the things he'd said to me in anger, all of which were true? Truly, it was Leah who was punished, and by mistake too, and when I thought of this, I was sad all over again, marooned in my coupé, moving north through this vast continent because I was wilful and adventurous and I wouldn't give up what I wanted.

Crossing the river

And then, at last, I arrived, and there he was, waiting on the platform, which wasn't even a platform, but a mound to step down onto. By now I was mad for him to make sense of the journey for me, to grab me up and tell me things I'd never thought of that way before. But instead he was saying, Did you not receive my telegram? and, Perhaps you aren't aware? And by the time I was loaded with my things into his jalopy, I was full of pity for myself, and close to tears too, which was a thing I knew he hated in a woman.

There were to be two nights and a day together, said he as we bumped along, and then he'd have to be off for a fortnight, and no, he couldn't take me with him, what was I thinking? I'd have to stay in the house with the servants, but it was no place for a white woman and no place for a holiday either.

I just sat beside him, hanging on to the strap with both hands, because the road wasn't a road at all, just tracks in the dust. And not once had he touched me except to hand me up into the jalopy. And I didn't need his warnings about white women and so forth to know that he didn't want me there at all. I was his girl at the port, two or three times a year. And I felt stupid now for the distance I'd traveled, and all the letters I'd sent, the things I'd thought he'd want to hear about me.

Are you cross? said he, smiling at last, a hand coming over to take mine. But I didn't like this either, the smile brought on by my setting myself against him. And so I told him this, and loudly, too, and it was then that he laughed, and stopped the jalopy, and pulled me over to him. I didn't pout, that was never my way, but even though it was lovely to have the smell of him again, and the bitter taste of his tobacco, still I was calculating when the next ship would sail south from Beira, thinking I'd plumb for that, it would be a lovely way to go back.

It was sundown when we arrived at his house, with a great hallooing and the natives running out to stare at me. One woman stood apart, with a half-breed child strapped to her back and another standing at her side. He said something to her in her language, and she stepped forward, looking down at the ground. I knew then that the children must be his, and the mother suffering to see me. She was very black and smooth, with gleaming, round, full breasts and a beaded cloth tied around her hips. And the thought of them together filled me with longing.

He must have known this, because he took me inside, had everything off me at once, even the pins out of my hair. It was dark in the house, hardly a house at all really, just two rooms and a roof made with mud and wooden poles and thatching. It smelled of earth and animal skins and the primus and his tobacco. He hooked up the cloths that closed off the bedroom from the verandah, letting in the last of the afternoon light.

Come, said he, leading me naked out onto the verandah and pointing to a watering hole down the hill, the animals coming in to drink, this kind and that kind, which I pretended to see, but all I could think of was him behind me, breathing on my hair, the salt of his arm when I licked it, and how two things could be felt at once, one for this night and the next, and the other for my future without him in it.

֍

The first thing I did when he left was to make friends with his children. The boy was sober, hiding behind the mother, but the baby was chubby and smiling, and at last, when I gave the mother a comb, she smiled too. The next day, they all came clucking around me, mothers and children, holding out their hands like beggars. So I gave them little things, a hair clip, a ribbon, until it got too much altogether, they were shouting and grabbing, and I said, No more, that's enough now. And the mother herself shooed them away.

Every morning she came in at dawn to boil water for the tea. I watched her as she swept the verandah, the beautiful cropped head, and the flat little ears, and then the haunches brilliant in the sun as she squatted at the wheelbarrow to do the washing. And soon it was with his eyes that I was watching her, and the more I watched, the more I wanted her, not for myself but for him, and him for me, and I knew I'd never want him as much any other way.

I brought more things out of my luggage for her. A glass necklace, a brown leather belt. But when she reached out to take them, I held them back, wanting to put them on her myself. We stood face to face as I fastened the necklace, and then buckled the belt around her waist. The skin was firm and strong like rubber, and there was even pleasure in the bitter native smell I'd always found so revolting.

She stared down at the belt with a smile. It looked wonderful on the brown skin, having no purpose there but to decorate it. And then, the next morning, she came wearing a little beaded purse around her neck, and for a moment I thought he must have told her. And so I unbuttoned my bed jacket and showed her mine, and she covered her mouth at the sight, smiling. I took a coin out and called her over and dropped it into her purse. And I didn't put the bed jacket back on again, but lay there with my breasts loose and free like hers. And every night after that I lay naked under the mosquito netting, thinking of her lying there in my place.

And perhaps she thought of me there, too, because one day she came in with a little gift of her own. It was a purse just like hers, which I put on immediately. And, somehow, giving me that gift and seeing it every day around my neck made her less shy. I could get her to join me for tea, although she would drink out of nothing but her own tin mug and sit nowhere but on the floor. When she took a biscuit, she nibbled around the edges like a mouse, and then fed the cream filling to the baby strapped onto her back.

During the heat of the day, we sat in the shade of the verandah, with me reading my old letters. I had found them in a small trunk next to the desk, neatly wrapped in oilcloth. And once again it was as if I were he reading them and also myself writing them, and now here I was, gazing out over the hills, with his woman and her child at my feet. And how could I have thought this up, dreaming as a girl next to the old aga at The Grange, when I was supposed to be peeling potatoes?

And when I'd read the letters and read them through again, then I wrote some new ones. First I wrote to Constance, telling her at last about the hunter, how I'd found him on the *Empress of India* all those years before. And if I'd lied to her then, and for all the years after, well it was because I didn't know how to tell her the truth. The hunter hadn't ever come up between us, and now she was a contented wife and the mother of two children, and who was I to interfere with that?

And then I wrote to Leah. I had never written her a letter before, and couldn't find a way to go about it without sounding nothing like myself. And so I crumpled page after page and threw them to the ground. And there the older boy picked them up and smoothed them out and laid them one on top of the other. So I wrote her about the boy, and how he had only ever used a stick to draw in the sand, and I'd given him a pencil and shown him how to hold it. And now he was drawing an ox or a cow, and I'd include it with my letter. And when I said that I missed her and thought of her every day, I wondered whether she'd know that I was lying. Because, now that I was here, I hardly gave her a thought. It was easy to remember the misery in the taxi and in the train, but I saw that that was a lie as well. It was myself I'd been miserable for, not her, the way life had got hold of my ankle and wouldn't let go. And if I was happy to be there without her, well it was because I felt free again.

And perhaps that was what there had been with the hunter right from the beginning, the two of us down there in the cabin and along the docks, free. And now here I was, and he was everywhere around me more powerfully than if he stood before me. Even the smell and the taste of him were not as true as this.

And then, one day, he stalked up out of the bush with his gun and his bearer in the middle of the afternoon, and never a smile when we first met after an absence, but I could see anyway that he was glad to find me there on his verandah, with my hair hanging free, my legs browned from the sun and bare, and his child playing with the hairbrush at my feet.

11

THE SHIP FROM BEIRA WAS FULL OF MEN making their way back to England from the colonies, all ruddy and roaring away at the bar. I might have joined in their play and their sing-songs, but as soon as we were really out to sea I was seasick. Any thought of food or drink, or even the smell of the breakfast trays coming down the corridors, sent me wildly to the w.c. And so I missed most of the journey and could only wish for it to be over.

And then, the day before landing, the sea calmed and I felt a little better, and could go up on deck. And no sooner had I settled myself onto a deck chair than a man came to sit beside me, very polite, and older than the others. He'd heard I'd been shut up into my cabin, said he. He'd suffered himself on the way out, but this time things were easier, and could I tolerate a glass of barley water?

He was an unsmiling sort of man, but the eyes were very grey and sad. He was a banker, said he, come out to consider the building of a railroad and some bridges. And so I asked about his family, and, yes, there'd been a wife, who'd died a year before, and two sons at Cambridge, where he himself had been.

And then suddenly he was saying he'd always been after adventure in his life and could never quite come up with it, even here in Africa. And I said I'd always been after a future for myself, and somehow adventures kept getting in the way. And on I went to tell him about my hunter, and my wilfulness in coming up here, and how thrilling it was now to be sailing home again.

And that's when he smiled and said, You're young and full of life, and I've been half dead from the day I was born. And he said it straight out, not asking for pity, or even for an answer, because up he got and went to stand at the railing. And I thought perhaps he'd climb over and hurl himself into the sea at the thought of his life half dead, but no, he turned and beckoned me to join him there, looking better already with his hair all blown out of place, and the nose like a rudder into the wind.

See the coast of Madagascar? said he. See the reef?

It's the sea I love, said I. I'd rather look out the other way, with no land in sight.

Well, he turned to me gravely then, just like my gentleman on the train so many years ago. And I thought, Any minute he'll be talking about waste and wanting a look himself. But no, he only asked politely whether he might call on me if ever he returned? And if ever I went home to England, here was his card, and what a delight that would be and so forth. But I knew there'd be no delight for me in going back there. It was here I'd come to find a future for myself, and here that I'd remain.

The ship docked early and I was quickly down the gangway. There was Constance waving, and Leah at her side, all flushed under the Panama hat. Back we drove through the racecourse and up to the hotel, Constance silent with the effort of driving, and me silent too, sending thanks to the Lord that there'd been no chance to post the letters—what had I been thinking? And then chattering for the sake of the girl, the presents I'd brought for her, the wild animals I'd seen, and so forth.

But when I gave her the presents after tea, a beaded purse like mine, a beaded belt too, well then a terrible heaviness settled over me, and I was hopelessly homesick for what I didn't have any more, or even want any more. And I couldn't help it, tears roared down my cheeks. She stood there helpless, torturing the purse between her hands so that I shouted, Don't pull it apart! and she started to cry too, and I flew over to her and wrapped her up in my arms and said, It's all right, darling. It's only a foolish old purse.

And so, by the time the newspaperman came home that evening, she was sitting on my bed while I told her about the hunter's house, and the hut full of ivory, guarded by a native boy with a gun. And then he asked her about her homework, and off she ran to fetch it. And that's when he told me she was top of the class in everything, and proud as could be he was. When she came in with the homework books, she held them up under his nose, chanting out the spellings, getting them right the first time, running off again for the test she'd done that day and the stars she'd got for it.

So I asked to see the stars myself, and she gave me one of those looks of hers, shy and proud, but also wondering, I suppose, what I would care about arithmetic. She held out the book to me anyway, and it was all sums in neat rows, and ticks and stars, and she was quite right, I couldn't have cared less.

It was as if they had it all rehearsed for my arrival, start to finish, the way they gave each other turns. But I'd never been able to stand a good girl, all the dark things buried away, and so I thought, She knows that the newspaperman is not her real father, but now, if she asks who the real father is, I'll tell her that too. I'll say he's a Jew, and a clever one, just like you. And there'll be no more of the lies the newspaperman concocted for her sake, the real father dying in a car crash and so forth. Oh no. Even her names would be explained, and the three people who gave them to her. Whether she liked it or not, she was mine more than anyone else's, and that I would tell her as well.

12

MEANWHILE, THE TYCOON BEGAN TO AR-
rive at the hotel quite often. At first, I thought he'd come to
start it up again with me and got out of the way as soon as I saw
the motorcar. But no, he hardly seemed to notice I was back. He
would shut himself into the office with the books, and then
come out looking very grave. And even though I knew Mrs.
Keane had kept things going very well, there was something in
that frown of his that had me hanging about, waiting for the
bad news that I knew was coming.

And so one day I asked, What's the matter?

He didn't look up, but said, Don't you read the papers, for
God's sake?

Well, of course I didn't read the papers. I had the newspaperman to tell me every little thing I didn't want to know. But
even if I'd listened to what he was telling me, people lining up
for food and so forth, and even if I'd remembered that I'd never
trusted the tycoon from the beginning, still what could I have
done to stop the Avondale going down the drain?

We were finished. The tycoon had bamboozled me from the
start, and now my thirty percent was lumped in with all the rest

of his troubles. And when the newspaperman came up like a man for once, and threatened to write about it all for the papers, what had become of the Railway Hotel, too, and who was behind that, well then the paper itself let him go the next day, and there we were, the three of us, come all this way for nothing.

In a way, I was glad of a change, as if I'd have to find something new to go on for now. There'd been a slowness in me lately, a dullness all through the days and evenings, saying, Hello, Mrs. Trefusis, and How are things today with you, Major? I hadn't been able to think of a way out. But here it was. We had to go.

The newspaperman walked up and down as I packed our things, saying over and over that no one would have him now and what would he do? And then Leah came back from school, and started her strangled little shrieks of terror when he told her the news, the two of them sitting there together like a pair of hobos already. And if I tried to shut them up with talk of the great good fortune of being alive at all, they just stared up at me as if I was mad or simple.

Well, I believed what I said. I had the money in my purse to get us a room in a boardinghouse near Leah's school. And I had the money I'd put in the Building Society, which neither the tycoon nor the newspaperman, nor anyone but me, knew was there. As soon as I found out how things were in the world, I went down to get the money out. And thank the Lord I did, because it had already dwindled a bit, and would have dwindled even more in the next few weeks.

When I asked for the lot of it at once, they told me to come back the next day, they had to do their calculations. But I said there would be no coming back, I wanted it then and I'd stay right there until I had it. And so finally I got what was left, all in twenty-pound notes and some change. And I took it home and sewed it into the lining of my navy felt hat, and there it sat on my head, or in my hands, with the crown dipping a little towards the middle.

And the next thing I did was to go straight to Leah's school, because that was one of the panics at home. And, when I said what I had come about, I was shown in to the headmistress, a squinty old cow with a grey bun. She sized me up, and asked me to sit down, please, *Mrs. La Grange.* And it was just as well that the girl was clever, because the old cow came up with a bursary then and there, even though she carried on about everyone being on hard times these days, the school as well, and Allegra would have to stay at the top of the class or the money could be taken away again. And so I told her there was always the government school, which my husband himself preferred, being a man of the people. And, if she saw I was bluffing, she didn't show it, but looked at me more carefully then, and said, Allegra should stay where she is.

When I got back to the room, Leah was alone, poring over a geography book. So I sat down on the bed and said, Look, my girl, there are things you should know about who you are, whatever they call you at school. And I told her about the old Jew and all his money, and how I'd gone to work there as a housekeeper, and how he'd come over the day she was born and given her the name Leah, which was her real name because it came from her real father. And as I spoke the black eyes stared darker and darker with the knowledge, and for a long time after that she was quiet, and sometimes the head would tilt a little like a bird's, as if she were hearing some music.

And then finally she looked up and said to me, They use our names as they're written in the school register, and that's why they call me Allegra.

And I went over to take her in my arms, and hung on tight. We would always know things in different ways, she and I. The Lord must have had a good laugh when he gave us to each other. And I was a stupid old cow myself.

13

SINGING WAS THE ONLY THING THAT
changed Leah from the grave child she was into a creature of joy.
Mrs. Jones, who owned the boardinghouse, was Welsh and
loved a bit of a song. And so she'd taken to Leah right away and
given her the use of the piano whenever she wished. Let anyone
raise a word about it, they had her to consider.

But no one objected. They were all tickled pink at the serious
little thing sitting there at the piano, her neck held high and the
beak opened wide to sing. In every other way, she made herself
small in the world, dropping the eyes at dinner in case anyone
might ask her a question, or scurrying along the wall of the passage like an insect if someone was coming in the other direction.
But when she was singing, well then she rose above her own
pride and became something quite different.

Every evening before supper, she practiced the song she was
to sing for the under-twelves at the eisteddfod—"Who Is
Sylvia?" The newspaperman liked to sit in the big armchair
with the evening paper and listen, closing his eyes in pleasure
from time to time. But then, when the day of the eisteddfod

came at last, she asked if we'd both mind leaving her alone to practice, it's what the singing teacher had told her to do. And so off we went for a walk, the newspaperman and I.

We were hardly ever alone these days, with Leah there at every meal and sleeping in the little alcove of our room at night. And so there was a sort of awkwardness to him, walking along beside me, almost the way he'd been in the beginning, except that now he despised me and he loved my daughter more than ever.

He had found himself a job quite easily after all that fuss, teaching in the government school. And so it was marking every night, and funny stories to tell Leah about the naughty things the boys did in class, and I thought that this walk was a good time to suggest he might ask Mrs. Jones for the room next door to ours for himself. And yes, said he, he'd thought of that already—although it was always myself who had to bring up the spending of his money.

As for me, I was back at the Avondale as manageress for the new owners, but not before they had tried a few others and found them drinking or stealing or sloughing off. And who was to say, it might well have been the tycoon himself behind it all again, because the new owners were another Pty. Ltd., I could never get a straight answer out of anyone, and he was still on the City Council, and none the worse for wear that I could tell.

They paid me the same salary as before, only now I took it in cash, and once a week, too. And when things got too much for my hat, I sat down and read the newspapers after all, and

Power failure

decided there wasn't a bank to be trusted. So I took out a safe box for myself, and put the money in there, and the key in the purse around my neck.

⚜

The day of the eistedfodd, the City Hall was like a Turkish bath, people fanning themselves with the programs and raising their eyebrows to each other about the heat. And so it was a while before I noticed the stylish little woman sitting at the adjudicators' table in the middle of the aisle, and my heart went wild with beating. I knew her at once, of course, the nose, and the eyes, and also the sort of frowning importance she'd always given herself, even though she was all grown up now, and with quite a bosom too, very smart in a silk challis frock, the face rouged and the nails varnished, and the hair in a fashionable wave.

And just as I was trying out a look of my own, something between a smile and a sneer, well Leah ran up to say she had to go backstage now, and would we stay where we were so she could find us afterwards? I had to pull my eyes away from the other to look at the girl at my side. There they were, both the same. And how could it surprise me?

Ma! said Leah. I have to go!

And so I took the serious little face in my hands and said as usual, Bless you, my darling, do the best you can with the gift you've been given. Except that I could hardly get the words out for the mad fear that Sarah would see us and come over and snatch the girl to herself. It had happened in my dreams already, and I'd cried bitterly for the loss, although, somehow, it was I who was being taken away, and where she was taking me I didn't know, except that it was against my will, and I was leaving myself behind as well, and that's why I was crying.

The pianist sat down at last, and, one by one, the children came on like frightened rabbits, some of them needing to be coaxed, some having to start all over again from the beginning because they had forgotten the words. And then, at last, the under-twelves were announced, and on came Leah in the white dress I had made her, and the velvet snood, and the cheeks pink with a bit of my rouge. She settled herself in place, and put the hands in front of her, taking her time just as the teacher had told her to. But the old bag at the piano got impatient and began anyway, without even a nod, and so Leah started up on "Who Is Sylvia?," the voice like a little bell.

I knew every note of that song, and every word too, all that palaver about Sylvia, whoever she was. Truly I was sick of it, and had never been able to stand the name Sylvia either. Nor could I stand the way Leah opened her eyes wider in some parts, and tilted her head with a coy little smile, which didn't suit her at all, except that now that she was up there, singing for all she was worth, I forgot about all that, and felt a wild pride, knowing she was mine.

And, of course, I couldn't help glancing over at the adjudicators' table to see how the other one liked it. And there she was, leaning forward with the chin on the hands, smiling a real smile for once. And when it was all over, and the newspaperman turned to me and said, I think she'll win it, well I opened the program, pretending not to hear, because the stupid fool had never learned not to tempt the devil. And that's when I saw the name there, large as life. Sarah Moskovitz, R.A.D.A. And I looked around, thinking the old man must surely be behind me, too. But of course he wasn't. There was only good old Constance, waving at me from the back. She must have slipped in late and left the children with the nanny.

After the singing was finished and the adjudicators had made up their minds, well then Sarah herself stood up and walked down the aisle, up onto the stage. "Silence!" she said in that voice of hers, which now had quite a boom to it. And then through the categories she went, up and up—highly commended, third place, second place, and so forth, handing out the certificates one after the other. When she reached first place for the under-twelves, she stopped.

I have something to say, she said. Our first place goes to a girl with such promise that we are awarding her the Beatrice Campbell Bursary for Young Singers, an honor usually reserved for the under-sixteens.

I knew it was my Leah who had won it, and searched for her head in the front, where the children sat.

Allegra La Grange, will you please come up to the stage, boomed Sarah.

Up went Leah, the eyes fixed on the floor. Sarah smiled at her and shook her hand, and then she leaned forward to say something, and Leah, red as a beetroot, gave a nod and looked up into Sarah's eyes. And it might as well have been the truth about themselves that they were agreeing upon up there, both of them formal, sober, proud and dark.

❧

Out we went to the foyer at last, Leah clutching her cup and her certificate, and people coming up to us with congratulations. And that's when Sarah found her way up, too. At first she didn't see me, thinking, like everyone else, that Constance and the newspaperman must be the parents. And so she held out her hand to Constance and was beginning on a rigmarole of how she had started her own elocution and drama school for children, when Constance pointed to me, and said, That is Mrs. La Grange.

Well, for once, I hardly knew what I would say and where I'd find the voice. But I managed, Hello, Sarah, it's me, I'm Leah's mother.

The name was out before I could think what it would mean to her, though she was pale anyway at the sight of me, the bosom heaving and the eyes staring, dark as night. And there was

Leah, looking from one to the other, and Constance, too. And what the newspaperman was thinking I'll never know, but in he came, saying, Why don't we all go across the road to the Majestic for tea? And Leah's eyes brightened at the thought, and she looked at me for a yes, and then I at Sarah. And Sarah nodded, her lids half closed, as if she would faint. And I thought, Here we go again, there'll never be an end to this.

Town on a Saturday morning

14

WELL, ONCE THEY HAD FOUND EACH OTHER, there was nothing to keep them apart. First it was Leah, beseeching me to find the money for lessons with Sarah. And then, before I could find a way to say no, there was Sarah herself sitting in the front parlor when I came in from the Avondale, and Mrs. Jones flapping around her as if the Queen herself had come to visit, with her smart shoes and polished nails.

Well, Sarah, said I, so here we are again. I was tired from the day and dying for a whiskey and soda. And so I offered to fetch her one too.

But she gave a little shake to the head. Is there somewhere we can talk where we'll be left alone? said she.

Mrs. Jones took the hint and bustled out to listen from the other side of the door.

I'll come to the point, said Sarah. I'd like Allegra to come to me for elocution and movement. She has a lovely little voice, but her diction is sloppy, and she can't move across a room.

She was good enough to win the bursary, said I. But the words only made her smile, because who had given the girl the bursary but she?

I'm quite prepared to halve my normal fee, said she.

And that's when Mrs. Jones must have pushed her ear too close, and the latch sprang open and in she fell. And there down the corridor was Leah herself, listening too, no doubt. Well, what could I do, with all of them lined up against me, wanting only what any normal mother would be willing to give?

And so twice a week, after school, Leah took the bus down to Sarah's theater, right across the road from the old synagogue. And afterwards she walked through town to Aliwal Court for her singing lesson. And now it was the A-E-I-O-U's as well as the scales and the singing, and I thought I'd go mad altogether with the racket.

Even Mrs. Jones couldn't see the point of all that shouting, as she put it, and asked if Leah could keep it down a bit, and only between tea and supper, when the others weren't back from their jobs yet. And so Leah found a way of suggesting that perhaps there was somewhere else we might think of living, somewhere that she could practice when she needed to?

Well, I wasn't taken in by the timid voice to get what she wanted, and to hell with the seven and six a month I paid already for all that racket. Where did she think we'd come up with another piano and another Mrs. Jones, I wanted to know? And what on earth had given her the idea that her particular future was the main point of it all for everyone?

And then there was weeping, of course, and carrying on, and Mrs. Jones coming up to put her oar in. But, for all the weeping, the girl was obstinate, and wouldn't be found in the wrong. That's not what she meant, said she, and I'd twisted it all about. And I thought, They're the same in this too, she and Sarah. That quietness isn't quietness at all, it's a way of holding themselves above the ones who make all the real noise, like me. And in the end, they exhaust us and they get what they want anyway.

And then, a few days later, came a note from Sarah. Would I come down to the theater on Saturday at half past twelve, there was something she'd like to talk to me about?

Well, I'd always been a good sleeper, but now I lay awake every night until Saturday, thinking of what she might be wanting to say to me and how I might answer to let her know who was who and why. And so, by the time Saturday came, I was as pale as can be, and my eyes all red, as if I'd been crying.

The theater was just a large hall, with some rooms off to the side, and one for an office. It was gloomy in there, with the chairs all lined up, and a boy sweeping the empty stage.

Sarah was waiting for me behind her desk, not bothering to stand up, or even to smile. And all I could think of was how she'd looked that last day in the mirror, because that's how she looked now, small as a bird, and the great eyes staring.

Is something the matter, Sarah? I asked.

My father's dying, said she. That's why I sent the note.

I sat down then, a whole new jumble of questions and answers in my head.

He would like to see you, said she, and also the child.

She stumbled a bit before saying "the child," not wanting to use the false name, nor the real one either. But the way it came out in the end, *the child,* was worse, really, because there it was, as simple as that, his child.

When? I asked, wondering how to prepare Leah for a dying old man as a father.

Today? For tea?

And so there we were that afternoon, Leah and I, standing at the front door of the old house, ringing the bell. She'd listened, as usual, in silence, when I'd told her where we were going and why. And then all the way there on the tram she was silent, watching out for the racecourse, and looking up at each house we passed until I stopped, and she said, This one?

There was the lace in the glass of the front door, and Sarah opening it to us now, looking down at Leah and smiling a strange sort of pickled smile, as if they had a secret between them, which they did in a way, and didn't any more either. Well, Leah walked in, straight and solemn, like a large black bird herself, refusing the hand I held out to her. She followed Sarah into the front parlor, where the old man was dying now in the same bed that the wife had died in.

He was looking out for us when we came in, but especially for the girl, and when he saw her, tears spilled down the old cheeks, all sunken in, and mottled, and stubbled with grey. He said something in their language to Sarah, who put a hand on

Leah's back to edge her forward. But the girl had come to a dead halt in the middle of the carpet and the feet wouldn't move her any closer.

She clasped her hands behind her back in case somehow he reached out for them. And there she stood, with me behind her whispering, Go up to the bed, he can't hurt you at all, go on.

But it was hopeless, she wouldn't budge. And so I went up myself, and bent over him and smoothed down the fuzz of hair behind the ears. And that made him close his eyes, the tears still squeezing out. And Sarah said, I'll ring for tea, bring up a chair for yourself. And so there we sat side by side, Sarah and I, and Leah behind, all of us looking at him, the ragged brown teeth, and the mouth drooling at the edges, and the bald old head crusted now with scabs and ooze. And how long we would have gone on sitting like that, I don't know, but suddenly he opened his eyes and started up in the whiny old voice, saying things to Sarah, and she translating for me.

What he wanted to know, she said, was what had happened to the Railway Hotel, and what to me. And in giving him the answers, I gave them to Sarah too, and to Leah, as much as she could take in.

So the money was gone? he wanted to know. And yes, said I, and I explained about the tycoon and his Pty. Ltd.'s. And at this the old Jew laughed. He giggled, too. He scrinched up the eyes and there were tears now with the hilarity of it all. So I said right out, the tycoon was never more than a business partner to me, but not for want of trying I can tell you, which Sarah found the words for, never looking at me as she spoke. But they only made him laugh even more, and he repeated something again and again, so that even she smiled for once, but she didn't tell me why.

What do those words mean? I asked.

A *bitere gelechte,* said she. It means a bitter laugh.

Well, I looked around for Leah, and there she was, still solidly in place, staring at him as he laughed. Seeing me look at her, he started up again, beckoning her now with his hand, then pointing to something Sarah was to bring him, his money no doubt, he was always giving some to the grandchildren. So Sarah got up and fetched the little leather box on the bedside table, opened it for him, and yes, it was money, all neatly folded five-pound notes. He took the whole bundle and held it out to Leah without counting, me looking from one to the other.

She stared first at the money and then down at her shoes and shook her head. So I stood up and went to her, put my hands on her shoulders and said, Darling, would you like me to take it for you? But she only shook her head more vigorously. And although I was trying to work out how much the money would have been, I was proud of her then.

He still had it in his hand when I went to say good-bye, holding it out again like a beggar, wanting me to give it to her myself. But I shook my head, too. It was hers, not mine, and if she wouldn't have it, then nor could I.

We were out of the front door before I remembered that I'd wanted to show her the view of the racecourse from my old room, and the tea had not been served either. But she held me fiercely by the arm and was hurrying me through the crowds to the tram stop. The races were over and the people pouring out of the gates. Look! I said. But she wouldn't stop. She wouldn't even turn her head, so mad was she to get away.

15

THE OLD MAN LEFT MONEY TO THE GIRL anyway, the same amount he'd given me for the Railway Hotel. But it was to come as dividends, which themselves came from the selling of tobacco and tea to the natives. It was Sarah who explained the matter to me. She sent another of her notes, asking me down to the theater. And there she told me that she was going to marry, and the old man had left her the house, and she'd be wanting a caretaker-cum-tenant, now that she'd be staying with her parents-in-law till after the wedding, and wouldn't that be a better place for Allegra to grow up?

Why I didn't hand the girl over to her then and there, I don't know. It would have made them both happy and set me free too. But I hung on. I said I needed time to consider. I said I wasn't at all sure that I wanted to be down there again, with two trams to take up to the Avondale every day.

She put on a frown then, and nodded the head, and said, Of course, I understand, take as long as you like.

But I knew, and so did she, that she had won. If I had had a direction of my own, I would have taken it. But I hadn't, I didn't. And so I would go back to where I started, only this time

I had a husband I did not want and a daughter fiercely set on a future of her own.

And when the first of the month came and we stood, the three of us, with our suitcases in the old front hall, well then a great misery settled over me. I went to sit in the old man's chair while the newspaperman carried our things upstairs and Leah ran ahead, squealing for joy like a pig. And then I heard her shout that she'd found the room she wanted, and of course it was Sarah's. They might as well have had it arranged between them. Perhaps they did. I didn't care. The house smelled of death as it always had, and the old man's tobacco, and the food they ate.

Every morning, Leah started up the booming racket, prancing and mouthing in front of the wardrobe mirror. And then, when I came home, she was on to the same bit of song again and again until I thought I'd go mad. And so I'd go up to the third floor with my whiskey and soda to get away from it. And there was my old mirror just where I'd left it, and the bed and the mattress too. And I'd sit down in there to remember the old chap, and try to bring it back, that powerful feeling of being so very alive.

But it had gone, and wouldn't be brought back just by wanting. And so I set about changing the place around, moving the beds into the proper bedrooms, and airing out the front parlor, and then choosing paint for the walls, which Sarah agreed to pay for.

Nothing I did, though, could lift the darkness from the

downstairs of the place. And even up there on the third floor, the lightness seemed less than it had been before. So I tried sewing new voiles for the lounge windows, and covers for the furniture in a lovely floral linen. I hired a gardener to plant beds of dahlias and poinsettia, and to seed a lawn back there as well.

Leah was as happy as I'd ever seen her. If she waited around corners for me now, it was to try to secure her own happiness by forcing some of it onto me. Wasn't it lovely to have all these rooms to ourselves? she wanted to know. And, Should we all go to the top floor and watch the races on Saturday?

And then, one day, she came to stand in the kitchen, flushed as if she had a temperature, and trying to stop a grin. We were all to be invited to Sarah's wedding, said she, and she herself was to sing a wedding song as the retinue came down the aisle.

Well, this was as mad an idea as I'd ever heard. And so I went down myself to the theater the next day, and by the time I burst into Sarah's office, I was wild with suspicion.

I won't have my Leah made into a laughingstock for the sake of anyone's wedding, said I. And nor will I play the fool myself.

The jaw dropped then, in real surprise. Agnes, said she, calm yourself, sit down. Do you want a cup of tea?

And that's another matter, said I, shouting a bit by now. I'll take no orders from you, nor ever have done either.

She sighed and reached for a cigarette. Why on earth do you imagine I'd want to make trouble at my own wedding?

Well, I had no answer to this, but nothing was out of the

question with Sarah. I'd always been a housekeeper to her and a housekeeper I was still.

Allegra has the voice I want, said she, even though it's very young. But if you object, of course I'll drop the whole idea.

So it was I who had to decide now, and break the girl's heart if I refused. I pulled up the chair and sat down. When is this wedding? I asked.

March, said she, so there's lots of time to prepare her. And she rang the little bell for the boy and ordered tea for both of us anyway.

And the family, said I, the lawful children and grandchildren? What will they have to say about all this?

But she just lifted the nose and said, None of them can so much as play the banjo.

And I understood that, one way or another, Leah would be taken into Sarah's world, and if the girl had been strange from the start, well she'd be even stranger now.

⁂

First there was her dress to consider. Sarah was fierce in her tastes. She was paying for the thing herself, and would have it made by her own dressmaker, not by me. It was nothing like dealing with Constance, that sweet old thing, and the bit of passion she'd put behind herself so quickly to get on with her wedding to the doctor. With Sarah it was choosing styles from special magazines brought out from England, and the material ordered from England too, and then the tram to the dressmaker for fittings every time we turned around.

And then there I was with the magazines, finding an outfit to suit myself, and drafting the pattern too. The style was simple, a dress and jacket, with the skirt cut on the bias from the hip. I found a pale salmon chiffon at Grenville's and a lining to match. Since the tycoon had come in and changed the way I looked, there was no joy any more in frills and flaming scarlets. It was a shame, but there it was.

I was trying it all on in front of the mirror one evening when the newspaperman came home. I didn't even see him standing there in the doorway, so pleased was I with the look of myself, and with remembering that I was not yet thirty years old, and had known what it was to be loved, and also to love, and although I had the husband I didn't want, and a house that wasn't my own, still I had myself to count on. And my heart was suddenly wild again with hope.

That's very nice, Agnes, said he. Is it new?

I turned, and there he was, all red in the face, and I thought, Oh Lord, let him not fall in love with me again, I couldn't take it.

I have something to tell you, said he, plunging the hands into the pockets and rattling the change around in there. Then he had to clear the throat and stretch out the chin before he could say, There's someone I'm rather keen on, and considering the way things are between us, I thought perhaps we could talk about the future?

I sat down on the edge of the bed then, staring at him through the veil of my hat. Of course I should have known that sooner or later he'd be keen on someone. Even though he wasn't much of a man, he was a man nevertheless. But all I could think of was my Leah and how she would cope with this. Who is she? I asked.

And who would it be but another teacher, someone at the government primary school for girls? He wanted to marry her, said he, and to have a normal life, and children of his own as well.

And what about my Leah? said I.

Well, he sat down on my dressing table stool and rested his head in his hands. I've gone over and over it a thousand times, said he.

I waited. Going over and over it a thousand times was his way with everything, even how to carve a joint of mutton.

And then at last he said, Would you consider a divorce?

Well, of course I would consider a divorce, but it was my Leah who would be losing him to another woman, not I. And so I said, I don't know what you're going over and over, but if it's taking her with you that you're thinking of, you can forget about it right now. She's mine and with me she stays until she finds a man of her own one day.

And so then it was baleful looks all through dinner, while he went over and over it a thousand times more no doubt. And there was Leah, perky for a change, she'd won something or other at school and would be getting a prize on Founders' Day. And he was looking at her so hopelessly that even she asked him what the matter was. And so it was I, after all, who had to tell her that we all had something to discuss after dinner, and could she put off the homework half an hour for once?

16

FROM THAT NIGHT ON, LEAH WAS FIERCELY
against the newspaperman. Nothing I could tell her would
change things about. She wouldn't talk to him or even open the
letters and telegrams he sent her.

Constance, of course, was full of misery for the girl, and then
balancing it out, always wanting to be fair, with feeling sorry for
the newspaperman, and glad for him as well. He had moved
into a little hotel room, and would be looking for a flat for himself and his schoolteacher just as soon as he could get the divorce
to go through, which was no easy matter as he found out. He
had to ask me to say things about him, the face all flushed with
the asking. Well, the idea was hilarious, but I did it anyway, of
course, as long as he paid the fees. And so, at last, he was free.
And so, I suppose, was I.

I wrote all about it to the hunter, but that wasn't the same
any more either. I didn't need to be writing everything down for
him the way I used to, maybe because I knew how he'd sit on the
verandah with the bottle of whiskey whether he had a letter
from me or not. And that he'd either read the letter, or he'd wait
until he wanted to read it. There'd be no pouncing on envelopes

and tearing them open for him, and probably never had been either. Every six months or so he'd pitch up, and it was as if he were a husband himself now, and I the wife of a sailor.

And meanwhile, there was Sarah's wedding to look forward to in the heat of March, and the Avondale to go to every day, with the staff quarreling and drinking and needing to be sacked, and then the bills to be paid, but not by me, thank the Lord. It was as if I was waiting for something to happen, but didn't know what. And the waiting had me nervous, because I couldn't do anything about it, I just had to go on.

And then one evening Leah came to stand before me. Ma, she said, and she clasped the hands together, and the cheeks flushed up as if she were about to sing.

Spit it out, girl, said I.

If Sarah sells this house one day, could we please use my money to buy it?

I looked up then, but the black eyes darted down to the shoes. And I thought, How clever she is, this girl, wanting to give the money back where it came from, and to have the house into the bargain, too.

But all I said was that her money would stay where it was, a woman had need of it, which is what she'd find out for herself soon enough. And as for the house, it didn't suit me at all and never had. I was there as the caretaker-cum-tenant, and that's the way it would remain until I found something better for us.

And then the eyes welled up and the lips thinned out as she stared at me in hatred. But I like it here! said she.

Well, I don't, said I, and that's an end of it.

But it wasn't an end, of course. Another note came up from Sarah, asking me to come to the theater one afternoon. And this time I didn't rush down there, but waited over a week, so that every night now, Leah looked across the table with a question she couldn't ask. And what they'd cooked up between them, I could only imagine.

I went down finally on my afternoon off, and there was Sarah up on the stage, shouting, GET OUT! I CAN'T STAND IT ANY LONGER! Well, I stopped dead in the doorway, even my mouth dropped open with the shock of it. But it was only a play after all. She was up there teaching a young woman to fling the hands up and toss the head back, both of them taking turns to shout, GET OUT! and so forth, until I couldn't stand it any longer myself. And just as I was thinking I'd go outside and wait, well then Sarah saw me and said, We'll take a half hour's break, and down she came into the hall.

And this time there was no, Do you want a cup of tea, Agnes? But, Let's go into the office, and me following behind her, still feeling, somehow, that it was I who was going to have to get out because she couldn't stand it any longer.

I have a proposition to make, Agnes, said she, perching on the edge of the desk.

Well, I had an idea what the proposition was, and so I said, If it's using Leah's money to buy your house, I'm not interested.

But now it was her turn to stop dead.

If I took money from the girl's father, said I, it was my right and my own business, too. And if I lost it with the Railway Hotel, well the old man had a good and bitter laugh about that, didn't he?

She looked hard at me then, searching, I suppose, for a trick.

And so I said, One of these days I'll be buying a house for myself. It won't suit me much longer to be a caretaker-cum-tenant.

And that's when she smiled at last, and slid off the desk and said, What about a quick cup of tea? And the voice was soft now with smiling, and anyone passing by might have thought we were old friends, she and I, not wrestling over the future of her father's youngest child.

She took a piece of paper from the desk and handed it to me. Written there was the price that she wanted for the house, the amount at the top she would take in cash now, with the rest to come like rent over the next ten years. But the place would be mine, said she, she'd have the papers drawn up by a lawyer.

Well, what she wanted in cash was just over half of what I had in the Building Society. I knew it was too low, and also too easy. So I said I'd take no charity, whatever was owing had been paid up long ago.

No, said she, not charity at all. The area wasn't fashionable any more, what with the riffraff milling around the racecourse these days. And by the way, the furniture could be included for very little more, she and the fiancé were building a house out near the university, very modern, said she, and modern furniture as well.

I went out onto the street, feeling none of the happiness that should come with a house of my own at last, thinking only that I felt left behind, Leah and me both, the two of us down there by the racecourse, with old things included at a very low price, and me an old thing myself one day too, nothing behind me but the bringing up of a strange child in a dark house that had never been home to me anyway.

And so, instead of going back, I took the tram in the other direction, down to the docks. And there I sat on the bench, like Constance all those years ago now, homesick for the future I'd once looked forward to. But it didn't help at all, and I got up and walked along the railway tracks, with the sailors hooting from the deck of a ship, and the Coloured girls in the doorways, and the smell of the whales, and the sun on my face, and a tug pulling a ship to the open sea. And that's when the tears came at last, and I leaned back against a tea crate, and everything was fine again.

Levy & Levinsohn

17

ON THE TRAM BACK TO TOWN, I HAPPENED
to glance at the old Railway Hotel as we passed, and there was
a sign, large as life: "For Sale." And, oh, I reached for the bell in
a hurry and pulled like mad, and off I got, and yes, it was for
sale, inquire at Levy & Levinsohn, Field Street.

And so I went to Levy & Levinsohn directly, with no idea of
anything but that the Lord was watching over me. And when
Levy or Levinsohn told me the price, I nearly died on the spot,
because it was even less than Sarah was wanting, and less than
I'd paid myself all those years before, although I said no such
thing to them, but chewed a bit on my lips, and said I'd have to
consider, and why was it up for sale at all?

And that's when they gave each other a look, and hadn't I
read the papers? they asked. Well, no, said I, I hadn't, nor was
I the poorer for it. So they told me there'd been a scandal and a
raid, and all the women carted off to jail. Worthy members of
the town had been named, and the place closed down and put
up for sale, which had nothing to do with the value, I was to
understand, only the price, which was ridiculously low because
of the scandal, and because of the times in general.

I was dying to know what had happened to the tycoon, but I didn't want to spoil my luck. I only asked about the Municipal Corporation's plans to take over the buildings and widen the road to the Esplanade. Well, they looked at me then as if I were mad. Why should they do that, they asked, when the road was as wide as could be? Only the tram lines might come up one day, which would be a good thing for the value of the place.

So I said I had to consult my banker and would be back before four with an answer. And I went straight to my safe box, and took out the money I needed, squashed some into the purse around my neck and the rest into my handbag. And when the bank manager asked for assurances for a bond, a husband perhaps, or a father, then I told him I had bought the place once without a husband or a father, and sold it the same way to buy thirty percent of the Avondale. And anyone could know what had happened to that. And still, here I was with money in my hand, which was more than you could say for some people these days, wasn't it?

And so by a quarter to four, I was back at Levy & Levinsohn with half the money to pay down and the promise of a bond from the bank for the rest. And although I hated the idea of owing money to anyone, even a bank, well it was the only way I could have the place back.

❧

When Leah came home from school, I knew there'd be a scene. But on I went anyway with the news. If it wasn't a house, said I, well it was better than this dark old heap, or even the Avondale up there, with all its airs and graces.

As I spoke, I saw the jaw dropping, and the blood draining from the face, leaving it yellow as can be. And then the screeching creature began to shout, No! No! No! So I flew right over and gave the face a loud slap, and, Who do you think you are, Lady Muck on Toast, to be screeching like the devil when you don't get your own way, for once?

And out she ran, up to her room, and there was sobbing and carrying on for an hour or more, but it was too bad. I was sorry now I'd ever taken her up onto the ridge in the first place. All that fuss over her at the Avondale had gone to her head. And now Sarah had put her oar in. Well, they could both take a running jump together, I'd had enough of them and their stupid careers too.

And that's what I told Leah at supper that night.

And what's more, said I, you'll be helping me run the place down there, don't think you won't. I wasn't put on this earth to be housekeeper to my own child or to anyone else for that matter.

Well, she just stared at me in silence, the eyes wide and black because she knew what I was like when the temper heated up, and the newspaperman wasn't there any more to put himself between us. And then, seeing the way she was trying to swallow the food she couldn't eat, I said, I'll buy the piano from Sarah, and you'll have the dining room all to yourself to practice in, and, Oh darling, don't be sad, it's the place you were born in, and it has all those lovely rooms, much better than a house, and not right on top of the old racecourse either.

❧

There were two more months before I could get the papers all signed, and the Railway Hotel itself ready for us to move into. The place was gaudy with red and gold wallpaper and flowered carpets, and there were wine stains everywhere, and the stale smell of cigars. Some of the rooms had been divided in two and had to be undivided, and I had the whole place scrubbed down, and the walls stripped and painted, the horrible mattresses and linen thrown out for the natives to take for themselves.

Every afternoon, when I finished at the Avondale, down I went on the tram to see how the workmen were doing. And when the place was nearly ready, I chose which members of the Avondale staff to take with me, old Naidoo top of the list, and the kitchen boy, too, and the breakfast cook, and two of the more willing houseboys to be trained as waiters. I offered them a bit more than they were getting already, and an afternoon off during the week.

And then one evening, when I came back to the house, there was Sarah, sitting in the old man's chair, with the head deep between the shoulders just like his. She didn't get up, but said, I wanted a word with you while Allegra's at rehearsal.

Any minute, I thought, she could send me to the kitchen for a tomato cocktail and some anchovy toast to go with it.

Agnes, said she, do you know what you're doing, moving the girl down there to that dreadful hotel?

Well, I just sighed then, because I'd always known what I was doing, even when I was doing the wrong thing, and that's what I told her.

And what did she ask next, as if she hadn't quite heard me, but, Have you given some thought to Allegra in all this?

And so I made a point of ringing the bell, and telling the boy to bring in the drinks tray, it was half past five already. And then I kept her waiting in silence while I drew the curtains all round the room, switched on the lamps, closed both doors. And then I turned to her and said, Wherever I go, Leah will follow, like Ruth in the Bible. And if she doesn't like the direction I'm taking, well she has the rest of her life to find another way for herself.

And that must have sunk in at last, because all she could do was twist the great diamond ring on her finger, and say, Well, if that's the way you see it, Agnes.

18

1 9 3 5

GOING BACK TO THE RAILWAY HOTEL GAVE
me back my hope. Hope was there every morning in the lists of
things to do, and the counting of the money in the till at the end
of the week, and then a train pulling in, and a salesman with a
suitcase in his hand wanting a room for the night. And, oh, it
was lovely to be in the middle of town again, and the rickshaw
boys yodeling, and Apple Sammy with his baskets of mangoes
and lichis and bananas, calling up and down the station platform.

I took my old corner room looking out over the verandah and
the street, and put Leah in her old room, too. The brothel-
keepers had bricked up the interleading door, which I thought a
good thing, after all. She wasn't a baby any more, nor was I
wanting one either. Sarah's piano went into the dining room.
She'd given it to Leah as a present, and offered the rest of the
furniture with it. But, except for my old mirror, I said no thank
you, I had my own ideas. I'd found an Indian to make covers for
the furniture that came with the hotel, and bought new mattresses and linen for the rooms, to be paid for over time.

As soon as I had the place looking fresh and new again, I

called on the newspaperman in his office. I hadn't seen him since he'd left, but Constance had told me he was back at the morning paper, his name all over the place these days.

And now there he sat in a cubicle, a little grey around the face, and the sleeves rolled up as if he were about to dig a trench.

Hello old friend, said I.

He looked up in terror then, as if the Day of Judgment itself had arrived.

I have a favor to ask you, said I quickly, and a small one at that.

And so he calmed down a bit and even managed to stand up and shake the hand I held out to him. I suggested tea around the corner at Grenville's because this place was already curious about me, with people finding excuses to walk past and have a look. And by the time we were sitting in the tearoom, at a little table by the window, he was glad to be there, and full of curiosity about all the things he'd been trying to forget.

And when I got to the Railway Hotel, he said, Yes, he'd heard I'd bought the place again, and the rubbled face flushed up with the memory.

And so I said right out, Would you write a piece in the paper about how I've done it up? And there'll be dancing on a Saturday night? And you could even put in something about Leah, if you want to.

And that's when he sat back and smiled at last, and said, I think I can do that for you, Agnes. It's a jolly good idea in its own right.

Upstairs verandah

And so, the following Thursday, I had the waiters all crisp in their white coats and turbans and gloves and red sashes, and fresh lace on the windows, and bowls of flowers in the rooms and on the piano. And even Leah was pinching at the cheeks to bring the color out, taking off one dress and putting on another.

When I'd told her he was coming, she'd stopped dead still like a praying mantis, staring. Well, I couldn't stand that look of hers, and I couldn't stand a grudge in anyone, and so I said she should get it into her thick head that he was a man who had loved her and left me, and if she couldn't be normal while he was there, she should stay away altogether. And then, by Thursday, she was like a bride, looking at the clock, and wondering whether he'd ask her to sing.

And, of course, he did. And smiled, and closed his eyes as ever, he couldn't help it. With a man like him, there was only one way of loving a woman, the way he loved my Leah. When the song was over, he turned to me and reached out his hand for mine, squeezed it gently. And, oh, I remembered all those years of friendly squeezes, and I thought, yes, she'll give herself up to such a man and never know the difference. And then up she came, shy before him, waiting for the compliments, greedy for them, like any of the old whores they'd taken away in the raid.

And so I said, Isn't it time for photos of the place?

And off she went, awkward as a goat, leading the way, and him following her from room to room with the camera, opening curtains and telling the boy where to hold this and what to do with that.

Well, I didn't have much hope for what would come out of it all, so distracted did he seem by the past. But then, when the article came out in Sunday's paper, the place looked grand, much grander than it was, and there was I, Agnes La Grange, leaning over the piano while her daughter, Allegra, played.

On Sunday afternoon, people flocked in for tea. They asked if they could look around upstairs, and so I sent Leah to lead the way. There was whispering up there, of course, the women giggling at the thought of what had gone on in those rooms, and I could only imagine Leah's face. And then, just as the last of them was leaving, Constance arrrived, without the children for once.

She'd come, said she, to join the celebration. But she was edgy and looking at her watch. And after a while I realized it must be that the husband didn't want her there at all, didn't even know she had come. So, to take her mind off things, I asked whether she knew what had happened to the tycoon. And yes, said she, he had been named in the papers along with all the others, this one and that one from the City Council, corruption all over the place. There'd been fines to pay, fortunes ruined, and reputations too, but he'd managed to leave the country somehow, and who knew where he was now, sailing about in the Mediterranean, no doubt, with some woman or other, and a Swiss bank account into the bargain.

There was a new bitterness in her voice, as if she was wanting to be sailing about herself, now that there was no possibility. And so I took her upstairs to show her my outfit for Sarah's wedding, and Leah's dress, too, and wasn't it funny, said I, to think that I'd met the tycoon at her own wedding, and he'd taken my hotel and given me a dream that didn't fit me at all, didn't suit me either. And now look, I had the hotel back, and without the newspaperman into the bargain. And, sailing or not, the tycoon was banished and I wasn't. And there was Leah now to say hello, and, oh Constance, I was glad to be here, making my own way again.

Sarah's wedding

19

Sarah's wedding took place on a strange day, dark inside and out with the beginnings of a late afternoon thunderstorm. Leah had been full of the wedding dress for weeks—the delays in the ship and then the arrival of the ship only three days before the wedding, and then the dress itself two sizes too big. And now here was Sarah, pale as milk and drowning in brocade, struggling down the aisle in the dead heat of March.

The bridegroom's family were dark as Persians, sleek and handsome too. The bridegroom himself had the face of a film star, with the soft brown eyes and the mouth full and rosy under a thin black moustache. Next to him was a brother who could have been a film star too, the long neck and the delicate curving nostrils.

The mother-in-law was a head taller than Sarah and every bit as proud. And yet lovely as she was, she was also miserable as can be. Perhaps she was even crying under that veil of hers, it was hard to tell because she was all in black, head to foot, as if she were attending a funeral. And I knew quite certainly that it wasn't the dead she was mourning, but the wedding itself.

How had Sarah done it, I wondered? How had she got the son away from such a mother? And who were they anyway, this new crowd, to be so blooming proud of themselves?

Leah sang from a little platform in the middle of the synagogue, without any piano at all. It was no wonder that Sarah had wanted her for the task. The voice was pure and sweet, and the song strange and mournful for a wedding, in that whining language of theirs.

People whispered behind me, wanting to know who she was. I was dying to turn and tell them, but they'd find out soon enough, I thought. Sarah's family sat on the opposite side of the synagogue, ugly as ever, even the blue-eyed nephew with a paunch now and a balding head. But there they were, smiling at the sight of their Sarah coming down the aisle, and weeping too, women and men. And I thought, They're watching her cross over, leaving them behind. And then there I was myself, my throat tight with tears, and wishing her well in my heart, even though I knew it was hopeless, she'd always be that girl reciting for the dying mother, and the father waiting for his chance to climb the back stairs to me.

❧

The reception was held over the road at the theater. There was a band playing on the stage when we arrived, and the hall all beautifully done out in arum lilies and white ribbon, with Indian waiters all over the place, and a seating chart too, in

Sarah's writing. I was standing in front of it, trying to work out how to find table twenty-two, when up came the mother-in-law herself.

How anyone can read that handwriting, God only knows, said she with a roll of the eyes. And, What's the name? she asked.

Well, when I said *Agnes La Grange*, she opened the big eyes wider, taking a look at the whole of me, dress and jacket and hat. My word, said she. My, my, my, you're not at all what I expected.

And that's when the bridegroom came up to her from behind and folded his arms around her like a lover. They're about to start the speeches, Ma, said he in a deep velvet voice.

She sighed then and gave another roll of the eyes. Darling, said she, won't you show Mrs. La Grange to table twenty-two. They can't very well start the speeches without you, can they?

And so he gave me his arm and a friendly wink to go with it, and there we were, the pair of us, walking across the hall for anyone to see.

And after the speeches, when the first waltz struck up, there was Sarah on the dance floor, tripping over the skirt, struggling to hook it over her arm. And then, when the music changed, and the bridesmaids' dances were over, well the brother-in-law took Sarah off for a dance himself, and the bridegroom came all the way over to me and bowed. And so there we were, wheeling around the dance floor, with him set free from the troublesome skirt, and Sarah pretending not to look, the chin tilted away from us.

How do you know Sarah? he asked.

I've known her since she was a girl, said I, I was housekeeper to the family.

And that's when he stopped and stared at me. You! said he. Oh, forgive me, I had no idea.

Well, I looked around for my Leah then. She sat at the bridesmaids' table, the spine stiff and the cheeks flaming and the eyes down on the cloth. She had waited almost a year for this night, and now here she was, waiting again.

And that's my daughter over there, said I.

He nodded, still staring. And then the mother-in-law couldn't stand another minute of it and over she came herself. Sarah came too, slipping from one brother to the other and hanging on with both hands. And so there we were, all of us in a circle, when the mother-in-law said, Do you go to the races, my dear? And Sarah gave out one of her barking little laughs.

And so the mother-in-law said, I'm dying to hear your whole story, my dear. Will you come with me this Saturday?

And although I knew she was using me to drive Sarah mad at her own wedding, I liked her the more for it. And I liked the way she took her son by the arm and said, Dance with your old mother, darling, for old times' sake.

But then watching them go off together, leaving Sarah and

me together, I wondered how I could tell anyone my whole story even if I wanted to, since I was still there in the middle of it. And maybe there never could be a happy ending, I thought, not even at a wedding, although it was all over the place in songs and books, and everyone seemed to believe them.

The races

20

IT WAS A BRILLIANT DAY FOR THE RACES, bright and clear. The mother-in-law came to fetch me at the hotel, and then the driver dropped us off at the entrance, and there we were, sailing in through the gates as if there was nothing to it. But, oh, it was lovely to see the people all dressed up, and the horses in their bright satin coats like the kings and queens of England. The mother-in-law looked like a queen herself in a deep purple dress and white kid gloves piped in purple to match. She led me through the crowds, and up and up the stands to the Members' box, people turning all the way to greet her.

Do you come here every week? I asked.

And of course she did, calling over a waiter when we reached the top, to order caviar and Champagne.

Where did you get the outfit you wore for my son's wedding? she asked, sitting back to take a look at what I was wearing now.

And so I told her, and also about the tycoon and his navies and ecrus. And she just nodded, and said, You're an apt pupil, Agnes La Grange.

And that's when I told her about how I'd got the name too, and she said she herself had grown up in the East End, a slip of a thing with no prospects at all, and now here she was at the races every week, and a great huge house on the ridge, and what was the point of it all? What was the point?

And so I told her how I'd watched the races every week from my room on the third floor of the old Jew's house, and sometimes on a Wednesday, too, and now here I was, and I'd never be able to think of it the old way again.

She smiled then, as if she'd had it all planned from the start, this way of getting to the whole story. But she didn't ask for it all at once, and I didn't tell. It was enough to be there with her, and everyone noticing us together, both of us laughing whether we lost or won. And I thought what a different matter it would have been down there in the stalls as a housekeeper with my pennies and shillings. And now it was my smart ecru-and-white spot, and the little straw hat over one eye and a glass of Champagne in my hand.

And that's when a fancy man came up and bowed to the mother-in-law and then to me. She gave him one of her smiles, the chin lifted and the saucy eyes looking sideways at him.

What's it to be today, ladies? said he. The favorite?

And I, who had never gambled a farthing in my life, took out a one-pound note and said, I like the look of that black one over there, number seven's my lucky number. And he looked it up, and said, Great Republic, twenty-to-one, not a chance. But off he went anyway, saying, Put that pound note of yours back where it came from, my dear.

And, just to show him, my horse came in second, and I said no, I wouldn't take the winnings, it was his to start off with. And he said, What rubbish, you'll take it all, right now. And so I did. And what's more, said he, I'm taking you both dinner-dancing tonight at the Majestic. And even though I knew it was the mother-in-law he was really after, what a wonder it was after the newspaperman and even the hunter himself to have a man say, Put that pound note away, and I'm taking you dinner-dancing whether you like it or not.

And then, when the races were over, and we were driving back to the mother-in-law's house, well I sat back in the car, feeling like a film star, going up and up to the top of the ridge. And the next thing will be the violins and the weeping, I thought, but who cares? It was just lovely to be in the films for a change.

☙

The house sat almost at the top of the hill, a great white pillared place with grounds going down in terraces, and a summerhouse below. I followed her in through a grand hall and lounge, out onto the verandah, where the husband sat in his bowling whites, making a great show of pulling out his pocket watch and announcing the time with a lift of the eyebrow.

He was shorter than she was, with English shoes and English manners, which was funny in a Jew, although he was dark and handsome in his own way, everything neat about him. He hardly gave me a glance, but smiled at her at last, saying, I presume you two had quite a time this afternoon.

Well, sure enough, she began carrying on like any guilty woman, laughing about my horse that had come in at twenty-to-one, and fancy that, and shouldn't we all go dinner-dancing tonight at the Majestic, it would be such a lark?

Well no, said he, it wouldn't be a lark at all. If she must go out, he'd go to the pictures, but if he had his way, he'd rather stay home and listen to the wireless.

And that's when I got up and went to look out over the garden, and oh, it was lovely down there with the frangipani trees all pink and yellow in the late afternoon sun, and beds of snapdragons and zinnias, and rockeries going all the way down to a lawn below. The view was even better than the Avondale's, with the whole of the Bluff and the harbor, and ships on the sea, too.

If there's anything as beautiful as a view of the sea, said I, turning back, I'd like to know about it.

But he was gone, and she folded up in the pillows of the swing seat with a scowl. It's always like this, she grumbled. Why doesn't he bury me alive, it would be so much easier?

And then suddenly she sat up and said, Do you play poker, Agnes? I have a game here every Wednesday afternoon.

But before I could tell her that I had no interest at all in games, nor in afternoons spent with the women who played them, in came Sarah's husband, dark and dapper from the golf course, and the mother-in-law was all smiles suddenly, holding out the arms to him, saying, Oh darling, Daddy won't take me dinner-dancing tonight, and I suppose you're stuck?

Well, I didn't want to be part of this game either, and so I said I had to be going, and, no, I wouldn't like a lift, thank you very much, I'd catch the bus back, it was lovely to sit upstairs all the way along Berea Road, looking out at the natives hallooing down to the soccer fields with their spears and shields for the Saturday evening fight. But she didn't seem to hear and nor did he. So I walked down into the garden and out through the bottom gate, and that's when I thought of my gentleman on the train, and all that talk of waste. Here was a woman wasted if ever there was one, with poker on a Wednesday afternoon, and the races every Saturday, and a fuss when no one would take her dinner-dancing. And so what if she was the beauty of all beauties? All her passion was wasted, her power too.

And, oh, I was happy to be walking down the hill under the jacarandas, the pavement mauve with flowers and the bus roaring in the distance, my own hotel to go back to, and two new residents coming in the next day, three the day after, menus to plan, and who knew what to look forward to in the future?

21

As soon as I was back at the hotel, I went to my room and took off all my clothes and stood again before my old mirror. I had set it up in the corner, angled just right, but until now I'd ignored it and the power it had to bring me back to myself. But now there I was like an old lover, the curves and the colors again, and my hands lifting the breasts because they'd sagged a bit, the hips a little fuller, and the thighs softer, and everything so womanly now, all the uses known. What was needed was a man to see what I was seeing, a real lover, not a childish fool like the one I'd just left with his mother.

Well, the Lord must have heard me, because just two days later in walked a trader from Mozambique, with not a word of English, but waving the arms somehow to say he wanted a room and would pay a month in advance. And all the while the black eyes were on mine, but not boldly, and I would have led him upstairs that minute except that old Naidoo was there, taking it all in with his muddy snake eyes, and making a show of calling the boy to fetch the suitcase. And so I just smiled a little, and led the procession to his room.

It was my old room, down at the back, with the little window out onto the alley. I handed him the key and pointed to the meal times written behind the door, and then to the w.c. and the bathroom across the passage. He nodded, never taking his eyes from mine, longing, I knew, to let them take in the rest of me.

That evening, he watched me from his corner of the dining room as I went in and out of the kitchen, and afterwards, in the lounge, while I talked to Mrs. Didcot, my new resident, about the summer storms and the husband who'd died, and the price of crochet sheen going up. It was lovely being watched like that again, every lift of the arm and turn of the chin, and then kissing my daughter good-night.

And when, at last, Mrs. Didcot packed away her doily and creaked off upstairs, that's when he stood himself, hopelessly stuck between staying and going. And it was just as well there was no language between us, because he could have spoiled it by saying something tricky or stupid. But out he went, hesitating first at the foot of the stairs and then again at the landing.

And when I'd done my locking up, and was climbing the stairs myself, there he was, standing in his doorway, with the dark room behind him, and only a candle burning. And so down I went and in I walked without a word, and he closed the door softly behind me.

He was small and dark, with a head of thick black hair and deft little hands that started on the buttons at the back of my blouse, the lips soft on my neck. And when he came to my purse, he just lifted it over my head, and hung it on the bedpost like a sock. And because there was no use for language between us, there were no thoughts needing words for themselves either. And so we were silent except for the sighs and the breathing, a man and a woman, that simple. And there we were in the candlelight, on my old bed, in my old room, in my own hotel.

The next morning he gave me a careful smile over his bacon and eggs, understanding, without being told, that whatever there was between us was to be a secret. And then off he went to do whatever he'd come here to do, and on I went with my accounts.

❧

It would be a long while before I could stop paying back what I'd borrowed from the bank, but the hotel was half full already, and I had a little band come in on Saturday nights again, playing only for the tips, and the bar was wild with men.

And then, one day, the newspaperman telephoned to say he was to do another article, but it would be about me this time, my whole story. And over he came with the pad and pencil to ask me things. And this time it wasn't blushing and clearing the throat, but with little questions all lined up. Where was I born? And, Why did I leave home? And, How did I come to be in the hotel business?

I had a lovely time making up the answers. I was a girl born with a longing to travel, said I, and a love of warm weather too. There were the summers spent in Brighton, which gave me a

taste for hotels. And if my daughter had been born with a talent—winning first prize at the eistedfodd and a concert coming
up at the City Hall—well my own mother was well known in
the music halls of England. And my father had played the
trumpet.

Never once did the newspaperman smile. He just scribbled
on the pad as if he believed every word. And when the article
came out in the Sunday paper, I glued it into the scrapbook I
kept on the table in the lounge. And there I liked to read it over
every now and then. It was like counting the money in my
purse. It made me happy.

22

ONE WEDNESDAY AFTERNOON, AS I WAS
haranguing Naidoo about locking up the liquor, who should
saunter through the door like the fairy godmother herself but
the mother-in-law. It was months since that day at her house,
and now here she was saying she'd seen the article in the paper,
and did I want to go with her to an auction, one of the old homes
up on the ridge was being broken up?

Well, I shook my head. It would be a while, said I, before I'd
be thinking of buying anything I didn't need.

But there'll be marvelous bargains! said she, frowning like a
child, and, Haven't you ever been to an auction before?

No, said I, I hadn't, nor was I much taken with the idea
either. It seemed a bit like horse racing to me. A price was a
price, after all.

Well, she took off into the lounge, saying horse racing was
quite a different matter, you didn't win the horse itself, and
wouldn't it be nice to have a settee here and a picture there,
although the place was surprisingly charming. She stopped
before a small mirror in a gilt frame and adjusted her hat with a

tilt of the chin and a purse of the lips. And how would she take
to growing old, I wondered? And who would get the blame
then?

She frowned down at her watch and said she must be going,
and what had I decided? And that's when I thought, She likes
to have her own way, and so do I, there's that much life in both
of us. And so I said, I just need to rush upstairs and put on
something decent.

And when I asked in the motorcar where the auction was to
take place, she cupped a hand around one ear and said, Surely
you've noticed I'm a little deaf? I've been deaf since I was a girl.
My brother Albert ducked me in the sea at Brighton and I've
never been the same since. She sighed then, the eyes fluttering a
bit and an arm flung back over the seat. Every year, said she, I
have to go overseas for fenestrations.

Well, she wasn't much of an actress. I could see she was glad
to have these fenestrations, whatever they were, to carry her
overseas, and proud, too, of being beautiful and deaf at the same
time.

And she was right about the auction. There were bargains to
be had, and it was thrilling to win even a footstool, and a little
painting of a girl and a dog. And then she herself bought me a
clock for the wall, which they were giving away, said she, she'd
have taken it for herself but she had too many already, ticking
away the hours and the days. And as for her daughters-in-law,
they hadn't a clue, either of them. Sarah went in for all this

modern stuff, chromium plate, so cold and ugly to look at. And the new one, that shopgirl, well it was ball-and-claw and a little box of a house to hell and gone in the hills.

I was glad about the daughters-in-law. It was better than any article in the newspaper to be walking around the old home with her myself, and the ladies of the town seeing us together, and me with the money to spend on footstools and paintings.

And when she said the husband was in a bowls tournament and where should we go now, I suggested a little tearoom I knew down at the docks. I liked to go there and walk about, said I, it cheered me up.

And that's when she really gave me a look and said, I think we're going to have to find you a husband, Agnes. You're going a bit mad, you know?

Well, she was too high up on the hill to want to go down again now herself. And so off we went, driving up the coast to the Umgeni Beach Hotel for tea, and there we were, sitting out on the terrace under a striped umbrella, with the sea all chopped into white horses, and the lighthouse and the beach below.

And then down we climbed to the sand, with her giggling like a schoolgirl and looking around to see who might be watching. And off came our stockings and shoes, and the sand was beautifully cool from high tide. We walked along to the end of the beach, and then back again, and when the wind suddenly took her hat off and blew it into the waves, she screamed with laughter, shouting, Good riddance to bad rubbish! And I could see what the men would love in such a woman. It wasn't only the beauty of her, but also the way she was caught, and yet loved to be free, needing only a little leading, and then there'd be no catching her, and that was what did it, too.

23

WHEN WE CAME BACK TO THE HOTEL WITH
our feet bare and sandy, there was Naidoo wringing his hands
and gabbling about a gentleman who'd been waiting in the
lounge for more than an hour, and then the gentleman himself
standing up, saying, I don't expect you'll remember me, and, I've
had a devil of a time tracking you down.

Well, of course I remembered him. He was the banker on the
ship from Beira. And now here he was with his gold watch
chain and his polished English shoes, unsettling old Naidoo
with his gentlemanly ways.

You'll never guess where we've been walking, said the
mother-in-law, dancing a bit on the toes.

And then Leah slammed through the front door, home from
school, and mumbled her way past to sing at the piano, and the
mother-in-law called after her to sing something jolly for us all.

And so the banker must have thought that life here was a
holiday of women, free and happy. In came the clock and the
footstool with the driver, and the mother-in-law said, Why
don't we hang the clock now? And so he stood back, smiling,
while we showed off for him, arguing about whether it should

go in the corner, where it would be lost, or against the far wall, where it would take over.

And when she left to fetch the husband from his bowls tournament, giving me a wink and a glance in the banker's direction, well he took my hand as if we'd been walking on the beach ourselves, and said, I'm at the Majestic, Agnes. Won't you join me there for dinner tonight?

But that's when the trader came in, the smile freezing on his face, and enough words of English now to hear me say how glad I was to see the banker again after all this time, and I'd rather come to lunch the next day, if it was all the same to him.

❧

Well, it poured all through lunch, pelting down onto the glass ceiling of the Palm Court and never giving up. So we couldn't go out walking along the Esplanade, which would have been a good place, to hear what he'd come all this way to tell me.

And all the while he spoke—the house he might buy if he felt like it, the books he might read, now that he had retired—well the head was tilting and the nose pointing in my direction. And I thought, Lord help me, but he's come all this way for nothing.

And so I told him where we would have walked if it wasn't raining, the yacht basin, and the ships down farther, and how, one day, I'd like to branch out and own a ship myself maybe.

Palm Court

And that's when he sat forward and said, What sort of ship, Agnes? Cargo or passenger?

But until I'd heard the words out of my own mouth, I hadn't even thought of wanting a ship really. And now there it was, as if right from the start it was ships I'd been after, not a house and a husband at all.

Generally one didn't own a ship as such, said he, or even a bit of a ship, but shares in a shipping company.

And I laughed then and said it was just a dream of mine, something to hang on to for the future, like the purse I wore around my neck, even now.

Well, he just smiled back in his chair then, with the pipe between the teeth, thinking, no doubt, that he himself could do much better for me than any purse around my neck.

And how could I tell him it was impossible to think of a man like him wanting a woman like me in any way that would have her wanting him back? He'd take over all my hope for myself, his sort of man, granting me what he thought I wanted, which would only leave me wanting what he couldn't give.

And so what did I want after all? Even the trader was growing tiresome. Every night as I walked up the stairs, there he'd be at his door like a little dog, waiting. And in I went, or on to my own room, whatever I felt like. And this didn't please me either. So what did I want indeed but to be mastered myself and yet mistress of myself at the same time? It was hopeless.

And yet here was the banker now, sucking on that pipe, and there was the lovely smoke of it, like the smell of the old Jew coming up the back stairs to my room. And I thought, There are worse things in life, I suppose, than being given what one wants.

✍

The rain stopped and I wanted a walk on my own in the fresh air. And so I told the banker I had things to do at the hotel and things to do on the way there, too, and, yes, he should call in the morning. And out I went onto the wet pavement, steaming now after the rain. I made my way to the Esplanade, and down past the yacht basin to the docks at the other end. And there they were, the Coloured girls and the sailors and the taverns, too, and nowhere to sit outside because all the benches were wet. So I strolled along the railway tracks, right down to the end, where I found a tavern I'd not seen before, and I was dying for a glass of beer, so in I went, and of course the hooting started up then, but I just smiled and took my glass and looked for a place to sit.

And that's when one of the sailors beckoned me over and moved along the bench to make room for me. And down I sat. There were three of them together, a bit older than usual, and speaking a bit of English, too. And when my beer was finished, they brought me a whiskey to follow it, and a beer to follow that. And when they suggested showing me around the ship, I thought it a lovely idea. So off we went, with the rest of them hooting behind us, and up the gangway onto the ship, and past a sign that said, "Officers Only."

The cabin was dim and still. One of the sailors brought me a glass of something, and another put a record on the gramophone and held out a hand for a dance. And so we danced, the three of them taking turns with me, round and round the cabin, bumping into things, and as the dancing slowed down and they pulled me close to them, one by one, so the laughing died down, too. And then there were two dancing, one behind me and the other in front. And the one behind was at my buttons and the one in front undoing the belt. And the third changed the record, and then came to join in.

And quite soon they had everything off me, and then the lights were gone, somehow, except for the red and green of the gramophone, and a little light over the cabin door, which was enough to make out one from another, the hands running all over me, and the smell of them, oh the lovely smell, and then one pulling me over to the bunk and laying me down, and me turning from one to the other, drunk on the smell of them now, and the places they were finding for pleasure, and my pleasure in them, and theirs in me, and all of us lying still afterwards, waiting to see what would happen next.

24

LEAH'S FIGURE WAS TURNING OUT BEAUTI-fully. She was tall and long in the bone like me, with a lovely bosom and a rounded bottom, and all there was of Sarah in her was the face and the skin and the hair. And even then, I'd done something about the moustache already, shown her how to tame the eyebrows. One day, I could see, she'd even be handsome, but she'd have to be older than I was, and pleased with life as well.

Now that the hotel was filling up, she wasn't allowed to practice whenever she liked, only after tea and before the drinks hour. And so she was like a maniac deprived of drink, running in to the piano the minute the tea things were cleared away.

At first, there'd been a complaint or two, but that was too bad. They could always go for a walk or move out altogether as far as I was concerned. And as for Constance and Sarah and all the others who seemed to think that the hotel was no place for a growing girl, well it was easy to see that Leah had no interest in the men of the place.

In fact, she hated the hotel, she had hated it from the start. But the maddening thing was that she wouldn't say so.

Whatever I told her to do, she did without a murmur, and then she'd come to ask if she could go to her room now, please.

And who was there to complain to? Constance was all for the girl, always had been. Her own children were little milksops, mincing around her skirts with their pale faces and clean hands, I couldn't stand them. I was strict about children in the hotel. I wouldn't have them staying, and if they came to visit, they had to go to the little breakfast room at the back for tea with their nannies. Leah was the only exception I'd ever allowed, even at the Avondale. But there she'd been different, lifting the little beak to sing for her supper, delighting the guests with the serious little face and trailing my scarves and bed jackets behind her.

Now she had her own ideas. There was the big concert coming up at the City Hall, and what she wanted was a dress with a neckline not too low, and straps not too narrow, and a waist not too tight, and a train not too showy. And, of course, it was her night, so I agreed to everything, although I thought a glimpse of bosom and a few sequins here and there would cheer the thing up a bit. I would even have taken a chance and done it anyway, but she examined every detail like a detective. It was as if it was more than the dress she was worried about, as if it was herself in that dress that was to be judged at the concert, herself as a woman.

And then one day I found my old sewing tin at the bottom of her wardrobe. I'd been missing it all this time, and wouldn't have found it at all if I hadn't been fetching one of her petticoats to measure. And then there it was, and I opened it up, and I forgot all about why I'd gone upstairs in the first place.

I sat on the bed, staring into the tin as if it were a nest of flies. There were bits of paper, and the top of a pen, and clippings from the newspaper, and hopeless drawings of her own, hearts and so forth, all of them like relics of the Cross, nothing to do with anything except Sarah's husband. I laid them all out on the bedspread.

I might have guessed she'd be one for falling in love with that sort of man, all gleam and polish like a tailor's dummy, but I'd been put off the track by her pride. And anyway, she was too old for this nonsense, and also too young and too fresh to be burying the bits and pieces of her love in a sewing tin.

And then, lying in the trader's bed that night, and him snoring gently beside me, I heard her come in from rehearsal and make her way up the stairs. Suddenly the screaming began. I forgot completely about the flies' nest out on the bedspread, and thought, There's an intruder in the place for sure. And out I went rushing, half dressed, doors opening up and down the passage, and everyone asking what the matter was.

There she stood, staring down at the mess of rubbish on her bed, shuddering and gasping for air. And so I told them all she'd cut her finger, which was a terrible thing for someone needing to play the piano, and sorry to have woken them up, and thanks to all concerned. And then I closed the door behind me and went back to bed myself.

Well, all she did after that was to grow more secretive, sitting silently through meals, glum at the look of whatever arrived on her plate, and pushing it around with her fork until I thought I'd force it down the gullet myself, except that there was the concert at the City Hall to consider.

And then, when the night came at last, and she was up there in the dress, white as a nun with terror, well she was only a girl after all, my girl. I saw the hands tremble, and the way she clasped one in the other to hide it. I may not have understood what was in the heart or the head, but I'd made every cut and sewn every stitch of that dress myself, and my own trembling was terrible. When the mother-in-law started unwrapping a sweet next to me, I said, Shhh! and didn't give a fig for the sharp look I got from her.

After the first song, and the whole hall mad with clapping, I glanced over at Sarah's husband, and there he was, not a man in love at all, but only looking around to see who might be looking at him. And as for Sarah—all through the rest of the songs, and when the last song was over, and the rumpus all around us, people rushing up to the singing teacher, shaking his hand and asking who the girl was, this Allegra La Grange?—well her eyes were brilliant with pride, as if she herself were taking the bow. And I thought, She doesn't know the difference. It's not mother to the girl that she wants to be at all, or even sister——it's the girl herself, the child of her father's passion.

Anyone want to go backstage? said she, leading the way to the front of the hall. And what could we do but follow? And then there was Leah behind, waiting for us with a bouquet of flowers I'd had the florist send around. And when she saw Sarah, she furrowed the brow and put on a false little voice and said, Was I all right, Sarah? Could you hear every word? But Sarah just smiled her thin little smile, keeping the girl waiting for an answer.

So up I went and hugged her and said, Who cares about the words, darling, they weren't even English. It's the singing that was the wonder, didn't you hear the crowds?

But she only blushed deeper and twisted herself away from me, and then in came Sarah at last with the praise she had been begging for. And that's when Leah glanced over at the husband, she couldn't help herself. And he smiled too, and gave a little bow, the eyebrow lifting like the dandy he was.

And then down in the foyer, who should be waiting for us but the newspaperman, all dressed up in the old tuxedo, which was shiny at the seams now and pulling a bit in the middle. And what did Leah do when she saw him but close her eyes and cross her hands over her heart like a dying swan, and then hold them out to him in silence as if he himself were the long-lost father.

Well, he just groped back for the pregnant wife behind him, a schoolteacher through and through with the homemade frock and the little permed curls in the hair. Leah smiled, all graciousness, and leaned over to brush the woman's cheek with her own. Thank you for coming, she whispered. Thank you, thank you.

Well, I cut in then, saying Naidoo would be wondering where we were, and would the newspaperman and his wife like to join us for supper at the hotel, we were having real Champagne, and lucky, wasn't it, that there was no school tomorrow, or Leah would have to leave her own party and go to bed?

She blushed at this, darting the black eyes over at Sarah's husband to see if he'd heard. But he was practicing his charm on the newspaperman's wife, all blushes herself now.

And then all through dinner, there was Leah at the head of the table, scolding the waiter for spilling the gravy, sweeping off to the kitchen and coming back with tomorrow's bread. And there was Sarah's husband, glad of the fuss at last, and the mother-in-law, taking in the whole thing with a crooked sort of smile. And I thought, Don't you size her up for revenge on the daughter-in-law, my ladyship. It'll be over my dead body, that I can tell you.

And when they'd all left at last and I was wondering how to say what I had been waiting all this time to say to the girl, she just sauntered out, leaving me to do the tidying and the locking up.

Well, I went after her, standing at the foot of the stairs, and saying, Young woman, you come down here this minute, I have something to say, and it must be said now.

She stopped then, just before the turn of the stairs. What? said she, as if I were one of the servants, or a beggar in the street.

Down! I said. You come down here this minute!

But now it was a yawn she put on, and then a sigh, and the mouth turned down with the boredom of it all. I'm tired, said she, surely you can understand that?

And so I started up the stairs, but just then she decided to come down after all, and not quickly either, lifting the dress and carefully one foot after the other. So I was forced back down myself, or be run over by a steamroller. And then there she was, leaning up against the banister, with the eyes half closed, waiting for me to come out with it.

And so I did, the whole thing, and her pathetic performance with the newspaperman and the wife, too, and all for the sake of Sarah's husband, a tailor's dummy if ever there was one, a fancy man, any woman's fool. And as for those stupid little things of his that she collected in my sewing tin like a sniveling schoolgirl, and the sulking that had been going on for weeks, well until now I hadn't wanted to upset things because of this holy night of hers. But let me tell you, my girl, said I, I'll go to see Sarah myself, and I'll talk to that husband of hers, too, if I have to.

And that's as far as I got, because, tired as she'd been, she suddenly leapt for me like a leopard, and grabbed my shoulders, and with such a grip, too. And, Don't you *dare* speak to him! she hissed. And don't you *dare* speak to Sarah either! It's none of your bloody business! And, Who do you think you are yourself? And, Where do you think *I* came from?

Oh! So that was it, was it? I wrenched myself out of her grip with one shrug and swung my arm back and brought my hand down right across the face, and then another on the arm. Vixen! I cried.

Trollop! she screamed back, her hand to her cheek and the tears streaming now. You and that disgusting man up there! I hate you! I've *always* hated you!

Doors were opening now, and, What's all the noise about? said Mr. Noyce. She turned for the stairs, but I grabbed the train to pull her back, and off it ripped, one side first, and two of the buttons flying through the air, and then the whole thing completely. And even as she looked back to see the damage, and I wanting to tear the whole dress apart now and her with it, I was reminding myself to use French seams in the future, and to sew in the lining too.

You've *ruined* it! she cried. How could you ruin my dress? And she sank down right where she was, and covered her face with both hands, and wept pitifully for her dress and for herself and for Sarah's husband too, no doubt. And the odd thing is the pleasure there was in watching her folded up on the floor like a great bird, crying like that. I just stood there, trying to catch my own breath. There was nothing else to say, it had all been said. Whatever was to happen now would happen.

But I wished I could sing myself, if only to see the face looking up in surprise out of all that misery. I wanted to tell her she could have any dress she liked, dozens of dresses much better than this one, and I'd never argue about a neckline or anything else either.

But I just reached down for the train on the floor, and put it over my arm, and climbed around her, up to my room.

25

THE BANKER WAS A PATIENT MAN, POLITE too, sitting in the lounge with the legs crossed and the pipe and the newspaper while I counted the cutlery and went over the menus with Naidoo for the following day. And if Mrs. Didcot or one of the others came in and started up a conversation, well he just folded away the paper and sat back to listen with a smile. Only when the trader himself stormed in one evening and held me hard around the arm, his eyes wild with drink and the fact that I never went to his room any more, well then the banker stood up to ask if I needed assistance.

But I'd already shaken myself free, and walked through to the hall, pulled out the accounts book and added up what the trader still owed me. I wrote it out on an invoice, which even he could understand, and handed it to him, pointing to the total. Then I called in Naidoo, and told him that the trader would be leaving, and please to send the boy up for the suitcases in half an hour. And if there was any trouble, Captain Culverwell, who spoke a little Portuguese from all his years on the ships, was to be called down to help.

And after all, Captain Culverwell did need to be called

down, and what the trader told him, I could only imagine, but he paid all right, and then he left. And the banker and I went out to a late supper at the Causerie.

He didn't ask me about the trader, he didn't have to, I suppose. But when we went to dance between courses, he pulled me a little closer than usual, and said into my hair, Agnes, I'm glad he's gone away.

It was a question, of course, but I was not ready to answer it. There was a lot I'd told him, and a lot he knew from watching. And whether he thought he'd take the trader's place, and how he thought he'd manage that, I had no idea. Dancing was as close as we'd come to an embrace.

And as we went round and round, and me a little tipsy with the sherry, I tried the thought of what it would be like, life with a man like this. But I couldn't imagine it. If he needed me for adventure, well I needed to be free to give it. And so what if I had a house in the hills with a view of the sea, and even a ship or two? Still, there was the man himself to want, breakfasts and lunches and dinners.

He smelled of soap and hair oil, and his hand was dry around mine. In a book, this would have been the end of the story, him smiling down at me, waiting for the answer everyone knew I would give him. But for me there was still the desire for a future of my own making. And if I didn't know what it was to be, or how, still I knew for sure, looking up into those neatly clipped nostrils, that it couldn't be with him.

And somehow, as usual, he knew all this without having to

be told, because, back at the table, he mentioned a thatched cottage he'd found inland, up in the hills, where the weather was cooler, more to his taste. It was suitable for himself and a few servants, said he, with a lovely garden that went down to a river, and he thought he might just buy it. And what was wrong with me now that I was suddenly wishing such a cottage for myself, but without him in it?

Aren't you hungry, my dear? he asked as I stared past him into the mirror that ran along one wall, making the place look twice the size. The Causerie was the most expensive restaurant in town, with the most expensive people, and there they were in the mirror, and there I was, too, like a stake sticking out of the water. I tried to tell myself that it was a long way I'd come from the room above the racecourse, but all I was thinking was that I didn't like the place at all, and I didn't like the people either.

And that's when I saw the mother-in-law smiling at me through the mirror, waving too. And so I waved back. And then, on the way out, we stopped at their table, and she had a good look at the banker this time, giving me a wink. And all the way home, I tried to tell myself that at least I hadn't married a stick-in-the-mud like her husband, but really I was rattled at the banker for driving his new motorcar like an old man, both hands at the top of the wheel, and people hooting for him to get on with it. He glided to a stop under the shadow of the huge flame tree and put one of the dry hands over mine and said, Agnes, I'm a patient man, I'll wait.

And then, the next day, in came the mother-in-law with news. There was trouble with Sarah, said she. She had caught the husband kissing another woman at the theater school, and bellowed loudly enough for the whole town to hear, and now the husband was locked out of the bedroom, sleeping on the old divan in his dressing room, and the baby due any minute, if you please. And all this she told me with the eyes bright as diamonds, and the laugh loud and raw as a hooligan. And, Can you beat that, Agnes? said she.

We sat in the window of the lounge, the August wind blowing through the cracks, and a cold grey drizzle coming down. Who was that man last night? said she, folding the long arms and legs. The one from the day of the auction?

And so I started with the ship from Beira, and the banker and his barley water, and then, before that, the hunter himself, and my jaunt inland. And if it was the error of desire that took me there in the first place, said I, there was nothing of the sort with the banker, she could be sure of that.

Well, her eyes were so bright with the story, and my own life seemed so thrilling in the telling that I was about to throw in the trader as well, and even a sailor or two perhaps, but she leaned forward with a little frown and said, Agnes, don't you want a normal life?

I laughed then, because there she was with her normal life, and what did she have to look forward to? Winning at the races? Another fenestration?

My life is quite normal to me, said I.

She looked around the lounge then, as if she might have missed the point. And sure enough, there was Mrs. Didcot shuffling her way over to the couch for tea, and Captain Culverwell behind, saying as usual, Nice weather for ducks, Mrs. La Grange.

Agnes, she whispered, leaning forward, don't let luck pass you by.

But I wanted to tell her how lucky I felt that it was my lounge we sat in, my tea and my scones coming through from the kitchen. It was only when Leah came in, sitting stiff and straight with her cup and saucer, the music across her lap like a shield, that everything seemed grey and old again, myself along with it.

26

THE CRIB WAS ALL DONE OUT IN DOTTED Swiss and ribbons and bows. Sarah sat in bed like a queen, in a lacy bed jacket, and the hair pinned up, and pearls dangling from the ears. It was the mother-in-law who had brought me here for tea. And now she was downstairs, seeing to the hanging of new curtains in the lounge, with Leah there to help her.

I'll be back in the theater in a week or two, Sarah announced, lighting a cigarette.

And did she expect me to argue, I who couldn't bear the childbed for more than two days? Before she could say anything to stop me, I reached into the crib for the child and draped the little thing over my shoulder, went to the mirror for a look. She was nothing at all like Sarah, a beautiful baby with a sweet round rosy face. And, oh, I had a pang then, remembering my own dark little bird and what she'd turned into now.

I put my lips to the ear and whispered, You'll give them no quarter in your time, my girl, you'll break their hearts with scorn. And around the room I went, pretending not to hear Sarah's suggestion that I hand the child over, it was time for a feed.

The bedroom was a corner room, large and comfortable, everything in it modern and polished and glassy. The house itself was in the newer part of town, not grand at all, and with no view to speak of.

Perhaps you'd like to help with the curtains? said Sarah.

And then in came the mother-in-law and Leah, the curtains hung, and the tea tray right behind them.

Sarah poked her head out of the pillows. Give me the baby, Agnes, said she.

But I took the child over to Leah instead. Look, said I, she's the image of the father.

Didn't I tell you? cried the mother-in-law. Didn't I say that from day one?

And so there sat Sarah, silent with her tea, and Leah too, and the mother-in-law carrying on about the beauty of her sons, what devils they'd been as well, setting off fireworks in the servants' quarters, tying cats' tails together with string, and so forth. And me finding a moment to mention that in the matter of children, it was all born into them, we were only around to see them through, like servants ourselves.

And that's when the husband came in, all dapper from the golf course in his plus fours and canary stockings, delighted at the sight of so many women in his bedroom at one time. But although there was a kiss for Sarah first, and then for his mother, and then a dashing grin for me, it was the baby he was really after. He came to stand before me with the arms held out. May I? said he, taking the child gently from me, looking into the little face with such soft eyes of love that it was impossible to remember the dandy who'd just come into the room. He put his lips to the child's ear himself and whispered softly. Then he nestled the little thing into his neck and smiled a real smile for once. I had never seen such a thing in a man, not even in the old Jew, whose tears had been for himself, for what he'd lost, and for what he'd given life to again.

I stared at him in wonder, and then at Leah, who was hanging on to the back of a chair as if to save herself from falling, and then at Sarah, who clutched her saucer with both hands lest the tea spill on her fine linen sheets. And did she know, with those sheets, and that bedroom suite, and the beautiful baby, and the beautiful husband, too, that there was no way to grapple these things to herself by force of will? It was not a play she was acting in, it was life itself. And here we were, all of us ready to see her taken down a peg or two.

Come, said the mother-in-law, let's all go down and look at the curtains. You too, said she to her son.

Well, the husband handed the child over at last, and followed his mother, explaining that he always came back early from golf on a Sunday because it was his chance to play with the baby while the gorgon of a nurse was off. He hovered in the doorway, waiting for his mother's blessing to dash back upstairs, but she ignored him, striding into the lounge, asking whether he didn't think Sarah's choice of maroon velvet a little heavy for the room, strange as it looked already with that wall of glass brick, and only those little porthole windows on the side?

Leah had planted herself in the doorway next to him, one leg unnaturally in front of the other, as if she were crossing a stream. With boys her own age, there was none of this lopsidedness. She was cold and superior with them, sailing past them like a ship, never laughing them off as a kindness, never teasing or blushing when they turned up at the hotel on some pretext or other.

Do you think the war with the Germans will happen? she asked him.

And the mother-in-law cocked her head too, and said, Yes, darling, are you off to fight the Germans?

But the baby began to roar just then, and Sarah called out to him in a fearful boom. And so off he dashed, whistling "It's a Long Way to Tipperary."

The house on the hill

27

AT HOME, LEAH WENT ON SILENT AS EVER.
What happened at school? I'd ask. And she would bend the
head towards the soup saying, Nothing really. And then this
annoyed me into saying, Nothing really *who?* And so she'd
murmur, Nothing really, Ma.

And so I'd say, You're still mooning over that husband of
Sarah's, I suppose?

And she would look up then, the eyes very velvet with misery, and I'd be sorry, but I couldn't say so. And anyway what
difference would it have made? She watched out for him now
the way she'd once watched out for me. She couldn't help herself.

Sarah seemed not to notice, or not to care. She was always
inviting the girl to the family dinners on a Friday night and to
the Jewish holidays too. She even sent the husband to fetch her
in the car, and to bring her home again. And on those nights,
the girl was like Cinderella going to the ball, rouging up the
cheeks and curling up the hair.

And then one day, buying material for staff aprons at The

Hub, I found Sarah herself, frowning down at the sheens, holding out one and then another against her piece of material.

Hello, Sarah, I said. What about some tea and a bun at Grenville's?

Oh Agnes! she cried, dropping the reel of sheen. For God's sake! You gave me such a fright! She clucked the tongue, and picked up the sheen, trying on the frown again. But the hand was shaking a bit, and I turned to leave, not paid any longer to put up with the bad-tempered little vixen. And that's when she said, Just let me find someone to serve me, and we can go.

And so there we were after all, walking down Joubert Street like any pair of old chums, finding a table at Grenville's, and me doing the ordering and the pouring to let her know I'd be paying for the tea.

And when we'd had the usual say about the crowds in town and the value of sheen over cotton and so forth, well then I said, How would you say things are with my Leah these days?

She gave out a little sigh then, and shook the head a bit and said, She's getting into some bad habits, actually. She needs a better singing teacher and she's not going to find one in this Godforsaken place, I'm afraid.

And so I said, With the life I mean? With the happiness?

Oh that, said she, tapping the tips of the fingernails on the saucer. I wouldn't worry unduly about that, if I were you, Agnes.

But the truth was that I wasn't worried unduly. I wanted to

worry her, and to warn her too. And so I said, It's not natural for a girl her age to be mooning about without friends.

Well, she gave me a look then and said, I didn't have friends either when I was her age, I didn't trust them.

And I said, Not so much the friends, but the mooning. There's a man behind it, I know that for sure.

Ah! said she. Yes. Well, she'll get over that.

So much for the warning. There'd be no nights spent on the divan over this. It was a shame. I would have enjoyed giving her a bit of advice myself, for a change. But anyway, there we were, together at Grenville's, and there was Constance, lining up for a table with one of her friends from the Ladies' Auxiliary, both of them come to town, no doubt, to buy wool and cottons to make tea cosies and tray cloths for some fête or other, and she had less and less to ask me these days, and nothing to tell but this.

By the way, said Sarah, we're taking over the big house in a month or two. My parents-in-law are moving into a maisonette around the corner.

I stared at her then as if it were a joke.

I'll have to hire more staff, of course, said she. But it'll be lovely for children. And a good place for parties.

I nodded, thinking of the verandah with its swing seat, and the frangipanis under the wall, the palms and the lawns and the view of the bay and the sea, all Sarah's now. And, oh, I felt left out of the great life then, down there by the railway station, making aprons for the staff. And so what if I had done it all myself? And what did it matter how you came to it, if you got the big house on the hill in the end?

Agnes, said she, there's something I've been meaning to say, although I hardly know how to put it. It's this: if you think Allegra would be happy up there with us, there'll be plenty of room. She'll be within walking distance of school, of course, and a bus ride from you. And you know, I think, that you can trust me to look out for her best interests.

Well, it was my mouth that dropped a little now, and even as I said, Well, that's something to think about, Sarah, I was thinking of Leah up there in the big house, and the hotel without her mooching around in it, no singing in the afternoons, and the little room she'd taken for herself down at the other end of the passage, where the linen had once been kept—what would it fetch now? And if I'd once said she would follow me like Ruth in the Bible, well now I said, Of course I'd expect to pay.

Sarah twitched herself straight at that and said, Agnes, it was my father's express wish, you know.

And that's when Constance saw us and came over, and Sarah gathered up her parcels and her handbag, and stood up, nodding to Constance and saying, Give it some thought, Agnes.

And when Constance sat down, well I told her the whole story backwards, starting with the old Jew's express wish, and finding my way to Leah's madness for Sarah's husband, two years of it already. And even as I was telling it, there was a thrill at the thought of Leah up there in the house, like the Trojan horse I'd read about, which I didn't tell Constance, of course. She sat there through the whole thing like a friendly priest, folding the hands as if she'd heard everything there was to hear in the world.

Oh Agnes, said she, it's quite normal in a girl her age to have a pash on an older man, and such a handsome one too.

But I just waved a hand and said, Two years is not normal, Constance, and nor is she.

She just gave me a look then, and a smile, and said, Agnes, my dear friend, are you sure you aren't a bit jealous?

And so I rolled the eyes, because she was always missing the point, and what had I expected? She was like a schoolteacher herself, the grey hairs permed in with the rest under the web of hairnet. A few years down the road, she'd have the ankles swelling, a footstool brought in to help the circulation, a spoonful of tonic at night, perhaps. And then, one day, the hand would clutch at the heart and down she'd go. And who but the milksops would be diminished by her absence?

28

THE BANKER AND I HAD FALLEN INTO A grown-up sort of arrangement. He took me out to dinner on a Friday night, and to concerts during the week. Sundays it was up the coast or into the hills. But on a Saturday night, when the crowds came in to the hotel for dinner-dancing, he politely stayed away. They were a drinking lot, noisy too. If I left them to Naidoo, or even to Captain Culverwell, who helped me out around the place in return for a lower tariff, the liquor was watered down, or there were cigarettes stubbed out on the piano keys, or the police had to be called in to break up a fight. And so I was always there to greet the guests, and to show them out again if things got too rowdy.

The mother-in-law was greatly on the banker's side, saying he was more than I could ever have hoped for, a decent man who would allow me anything I liked. I tried to tell her that being allowed anything I liked was less than I'd ever taken for myself. But she just laughed. Oh Agnes, she said, for Pete's sake, you've got an answer for everything.

And then, one Sunday night, I asked him in for a brandy. And because there were still a few men at the bar, I ordered the drinks to be sent to my sitting room upstairs. It was Leah's old room, next to mine, the door between them unbricked at last.

Earlier in the week Leah herself had moved out of her little room down at the end of the passage, and now it was as if a great stone had been taken from my heart and the blood rushing in. I was free to talk to the guests without the thought of that mouth of hers twisting up in scorn, free to have the banker upstairs for a drink if I wanted to without those silent eyes taking it all in and coming to the wrong conclusions. Her room was gone already to a widow on a pension, who told me that she screamed in the night and should be put as far as possible from other people.

But then, just yesterday, when that door opened down there and the crooked old thing came out, well then there was an ache in my heart, as if I'd thrown Leah out myself, pushed her down the river in a basket. And even though she was up there on the ridge where she wanted to be, well I wanted her back for that moment, now that she was half Sarah's already.

Sarah had come to fetch her, rude enough to sit out there behind the wheel and hoot, so that Leah jumped up like a little dog, and rushed through the front door, shouting for the boy to pack the suitcases and boxes into the boot of Sarah's car. You'd have thought the girl was going off on a voyage, so pleased was she with the sight of those cases being loaded in, and of Sarah waiting to take her away. And when Sarah rolled down the window and said, We'll be late for lunch, Allegra, well then she lurched over to me and banged the lips against my cheek. Bye, Ma! she said, and away they went, Lady Muck and her new housekeeper-cum-sister. And although it was a laugh, still I waited for her to look back and wave, but she didn't.

The banker stood with his brandy in the middle of the room, smiling around at the armchairs and the Persian rug and the little watercolor on the wall behind them, all found for me by the mother-in-law at one of her auctions.

Now I shall always be able to think of you up here, said he.

And I thought, Perhaps she's right, perhaps I am lucky after all. And even though I knew better than to take my luck so cheaply, well suddenly I wanted to reward him, to surprise him too. And so over I went and took the glass out of his hand, and put my arms around his neck. And before he could say anything that would change my mind, I led him through to my room, right over to the mirror. And there he stood behind me, awkward for once, saying, Oh darling, and, I don't need to tell you—

Well, I had to look away, not wanting to see my face as he fingered my hair and stroked the hands down my neck, the long thin fingers curling around the chain of my purse like a snake or a strangler.

I don't need to tell you how beautiful you are, said he.

And, no, there was no need, and yes, there was need too, because there I was now in the mirror, plain as dust, the clothes around my feet like a heap of dried leaves. And there was the banker, an elderly man limp with fright, and why I couldn't just leave it at that, but had to be leading him to the bed, I don't know, except that I felt blamed. I was to blame. I had brought him here for his sake, not for mine, and now there'd be a whole night of it, weeks for all I knew, until the thing could be done, if ever it could be done, and me released from this terrible gift I'd come up with.

The banker was hopelessly careful, nothing like the old Jew coming after what he wanted like a dog. For hours we labored on, with his soapy smell turning sour, the breath too, and then, at last, he laid a hand on mine and said, It's curtains for me tonight, darling, I'm sorry.

Outside, a native twanged at a banjo, and the tram rattled past with the bell ringing. I fell into a fitful sort of sleep, hovering around a dream of Leah falling off the trapeze at the circus. And when he snored, I sat up in fright, and there he was, lying on my pillow, the light from the street glowing off the ridge of the nose. And if I'd murdered him, I couldn't have wished more desperately that it had never happened.

Early the next morning he was up, asking whether there might be a spare toothbrush in the hotel. And when I told him to use mine, he just blinked at me as if I'd suggested he wear my dressing gown for the trip down the passage to the w.c. But he used the toothbrush anyway, standing at the basin in his shirt-tails, gargling and spitting, and then coming back to bed with new vigor, so that this time it was done in a minute. It was over.

He leaned up on one elbow, smiling down at me, wanting a smile back, I suppose.

But I was full of regret, even hatred. He looked like a horse, hanging over me like that, with the long teeth and the hair standing up on either side of the parting like a pair of ears. I turned away, pretending to be sleepy.

He stroked my arm, kissed the back of my neck. You sleep, said he. I'll let myself out.

And so I lay there listening as he pulled on the clothes and tied up the laces of the shoes. Everything was sour in the room, and in my life too. I even blamed the mother-in-law, wanting her punished for thinking she knew how things should be between men and women in the world.

And when he came to stand next to my side of the bed with God knows what ideas for our future behind the smile, how could I tell him anything of this, my dear old friend? All his desire was to have me for himself, and not in the future either.

He bent over to kiss my forehead, smelling of toothpaste now. And then he creaked out of the room, pulling the door shut quietly behind him.

29

1 9 3 9

WELL, THE WAR DID COME, OF COURSE, and men were scrambling to sign up and go off to be killed. Only the ones who were too old, like the banker, stayed behind without excuses. Others cooked up a crippled back or flat feet to allow them to prance around safe and free among the women left behind.

As for Sarah's husband, well he was the cleverest of all. He signed up for weekend service on the Bluff, with a uniform and a rifle, and no one to say he wasn't doing his duty.

It's not as if there isn't real danger involved, said Sarah, pouring the tea herself on the great verandah now. Every Sunday I was asked up there for tea, like the poor relation, and sometimes I went.

The Japs could send one of those submarines of theirs, said she, and then where would we all be?

Leah nodded, sitting stiff and still like a desperate widow herself. She was in her last year of school and had won herself a bursary to the Royal College of Music in London, bad habits or no bad habits. But with the war on, she couldn't go, and so here she was, mourning for the loss of her own future, perhaps.

Allegra, said Sarah, run to the kitchen please, and tell that creature to hurry up with the crumpets.

And up she leapt, and off she went, and for all the stiffness and the straightness, the spine didn't seem as proud now, nor the head either. Perhaps she'd looked in the mirror and seen a housekeeper there, not a sister at all. Or perhaps she'd given up on Sarah's husband at last, how was I to know?

Did she mention she'll be teaching at the theater school until the war's over? said Sarah. And before I could think of an answer, Leah was back with the crumpets, standing solid and sullen while Sarah made room on the table. And when Sarah said, I hope the syrup's hot this time, Leah just looked out into the garden and said, Did you see the air-raid shelter that's being built down there, Ma?

And so over I went to the balustrade and she came after, saying there'd be supplies for everyone, me included, in the case of an attack. And I wondered what had changed things between these two. Was it Sarah giving the orders, or Leah not wanting to take them?

The girl had come up here to find a family, riding off in that car of Sarah's without once looking back. She'd wanted a fireplace and a cozy life around it, it was written in all the stories. But this wasn't a story, I wanted to tell her, this was life. And she'd always be on the outside, with her private little ways and mingy little silences. She'd always be looking in through the window at what she couldn't have herself.

You'll need a new wardrobe, darling, said I, now that you'll be out of uniform, and, Wouldn't you like me to run up a frock or two?

And that's when she looked at Sarah, and Sarah said, There's a concert for the troops coming up at the Jewish Club.

And Leah said, We've chosen a style for the dress, do you want to see?

And off she dashed for the magazine, and there it was, the dress they had chosen together. And although I was longing to hate it, it was gorgeous, down to the ground and strapless, with a lovely sequined bodice.

I had Mrs. Fennels keep a pale green georgette aside at Cottam's, said Sarah. You could use my dressmaker, if you like. She's very good, you know.

But before I could say, I'll use no dressmaker, yours or anyone else's, in walked the husband, back from the weekend drill, all dashing in his khakis and boots and cap. And while Sarah was hauling herself up and saying, Darling, you're back! I looked over at Leah, and saw a dullness in the eyes now, the head bent a little as if by the weight of all those years of loving him for nothing.

❧

Well, I bought the georgette the next day, and the sequins too. And then down came Leah to the hotel, twice a week, for fittings, standing in front of my mirror, still as a mannequin.

Ma, she said, wouldn't it be easier to have Sarah's dress-maker do some of this?

And so I turned to look in the mirror, too, and there we were, the tall young woman with a straight spine and a long nose, quite pleased with the sight of herself, and then, kneeling at her feet, the mother, only thirty-six or -seven, with the golden hair and the green eyes and the pink cheeks of another race and climate. And anyone might have asked why the one was standing and the other kneeling, it should have been the other way around.

And so I stood up, some inches taller than she after all, and I said that I was there on my knees for the sake of my own future, not hers. And even though the money was rolling in from the soldiers at the bar, and every room taken, well there were other ways to spend my money than paying someone to do what I could do better myself. But if she wanted to hire a dressmaker so badly, perhaps she should think of using the old Jew's money I'd been saving so furiously for her future all these years.

And after that conversation, a strange thing happened. She went back to her old ways for a while, finding excuses to tele-phone me in the evening, or turning up after her singing lesson with a little present, a handkerchief, or a book she had found at Griggs's. It was as if she was sorry for me now rather than for herself, and the idea drove me wild with irritation.

I won't take any pocket money after I start teaching, she told me as I handed her five shillings one Friday. Sarah's paying me for the teaching and a bit for buses and trams until I learn to drive the car.

Are you to be driver for them now, too? I mumbled, crawling around her hem again with pins in my mouth.

Well, she looked down at me then and smiled. You're the one who minds, said she.

And so I did. I couldn't stand the idea of her fetching and carrying up there, and filling in on the nanny's day off. She was a fool, and she'd have a fool's life. And if I'd never measured my own happiness by hers, well still I couldn't stand the waste, and I couldn't stand to be putting in my days sewing French seams and sequining bodices for a girl who wanted a life of service.

The newspaperman was going off to the war, the real war, she said to change the subject. They lived down the hill from Sarah, not far from the old house at the racecourse, and she went there for tea on her half-days, and during the July holidays they'd taken her to the Playhouse for dinner with the older child, and then on to the fun fair for the evening. She was part of the family, said she, the cheeks flushing up at the thought.

I looked at her then, this girl without a family, and I thought, The old Jew has won the battle if ever there'd been a battle, which there hadn't. She was his daughter now, living with his daughter too, skivvying for her and doing penance for the sins of her mother. And oh, I wished then that she had the fire in her, the greed to have Sarah's husband truly, out of the sewing tin and into her bed. That would do it. That's what would settle the old man once and for all in his grave.

And then she looked down and asked about the family I'd left behind me. And I took the pins out of my mouth and sat back on my haunches and I told her what she didn't want to know, the cold and the dirt and the drink and the fighting, and the babies that came year after year. And no, they knew nothing of where I was or what I was and so much the better I was for it, said I. There was nothing left behind that I wanted back. We were born into a vale of tears and we would go out old and sick and naked if we were lucky. And meantime, there was happiness to be had only in moments, and those came not by wishing and thinking, but by knowing them when you found them. And if she was looking at me now as if she knew and didn't know what I was saying, then I hoped one day she'd understand, and although it would probably be too late to do anything about it for herself, there'd be the knowledge yet, and that was more than most people could lay claim to.

She stared down at me, all pinned so that she couldn't move, and I said I was glad she was living with Sarah, I was free from the way she observed me, day to day. And when Naidoo came to tell me the banker had arrived and was waiting in the lounge, well only then did I see, by the look on his face, that my tears were streaming, streaming, and the girl before me was crying too, turning her head away from him so that he wouldn't see. And there we were, the old Jew's child and me, in an old hotel, in a strange country, trying to make our way.

30

THE BANKER CAME UP WITH A FEW SHIPPING companies that would profit from the war, said he, while helping our side at the same time. Well, I didn't care a bit for our side or theirs, they were all men maddened by blood, but if there was profit to be had from the madness, and from the banker's madness for me, well I'd have it gladly.

I listened carefully to the details, and to what he said about the risks too. If my dreams of owning a ship for myself had been silly, well he never quite said so. He simply told me that an investment was an investment, and a sea voyage quite another matter, and, if I wished, he would stand surety for a loan.

But I didn't wish for this. I'd paid off most of what I'd borrowed from the bank by now, and could offer the hotel itself as surety against any loan I wanted. And this time it wouldn't be anything like the Avondale, with me brought down by the swindling tycoon and by the greed of my own dreams. What I would own in the shipping company was a piece of paper, an idea, a hope.

But I needed time to think. It was something new in my life, this way of owning things, this way of considering the future. And so down I went to the docks as usual, and there I sat, looking out at the ships and wondering how it would be, owning one of them. And, after all, it was easy to know that I didn't like it, that what I wanted was what I'd always wanted, the ground under my feet.

And so back I went to town, right over to Levy & Levinsohn. Remember me? said I, I'm after another building now.

And yes, they remembered me, of course they remembered me, and they were both on their feet this time, with smiles on their faces. But when they heard the price I could pay, well they pursed up the lips and shrugged and said, except for two buildings down at the end of the docks—

Where? said I, and, How much?

And so, by the end of the month I owned a building at the docks, with rooms over a bar. At first I thought I might give it a coat of paint, and new curtains for the windows. But then, when I considered the Coloured girls up there, and the rough use of everything, curtains included, well, I thought, what for? I'd bought the building for the future, not the present. And by the end of the year, with the money still rolling in from soldiers, I'd bought the one next to it as well.

When I went down there now, it was to look at my buildings first, strolling along the railway line almost to the end, and then turning up half a block and there they were, side by side, with the men roaring away at the bar, and the little Greek shop

The Lady in White sings to the troops

next door, and the Coloured girls shrieking with laughter or curses, it was hard to tell which.

And then one day, there were masses of soldiers on the quay, and a great troop ship waiting to carry them north. They waited about in groups, young men down from the interior, sitting on their bundles and bedrolls. A few of them called out to me by name, men who'd been staying at the hotel. If they knew they'd be back broken to bits, or not be back at all, well you'd never have known it from the way they were laughing and carrying on. But I didn't wish them luck and I didn't say, Look me up when you come home, because it felt as if the devil himself were there among us, listening to what was said.

And so I walked on, and had almost got to the end of the ship when I saw the newspaperman, in a uniform himself, with both children in his arms and the wife to one side, in a hat. And there in front of them was Leah with a camera, bending at the knees to get them all in, and shouting, Closer together, no, no, to the left!

She wore a little straw hat herself, with bright red cherries on it, and lipstick to match, and, oh, she was lovely in the sunlight right then. When she came to the hotel these days, the men might stop their loud talk and turn to have a look. But she ignored their whistles and offers of a drink, bowing the head and charging past on her way upstairs for a fitting.

Only once had she talked to a soldier. He was singing away at the piano when she came in, and she stopped in the hall to listen. Then up she raced to find me, saying, Who is that man singing Schubert down there, where has he come from?

And so down I went, and she too, following close behind. And soon both voices were singing away down there together. And I thought, Oh Lord, let her find a soldier to fall in love with and forget about that tailor's dummy doing his service on the Bluff. But when the singing was over, up she came directly. And off went the soldier a few days later, in a ship like all the rest.

I moved on before they could see me, she and the newspaperman, thinking I would stop for a beer at the tavern at the end before collecting the rent. For once, there were no Coloured girls out on the verandahs. They were all taken up with the men about to leave. And I was just at the end of the ship when I saw him sitting there on his bundle, half in, half out of shadow. The beard was off now, and the hair short, and he looked thinner because of it I suppose. He gazed out over the water, lighting a cigarette.

I stared at him for as long as I liked, thinking backwards and forwards through all those years, the days when the ship was in port, and then the journey inland, and his woman, and the little beaded purse that still had the smell of her on it.

And, watching him there, I was as lonely as I'd ever been in my life. It seemed to me a life I'd made out of cardboard boxes, and him passing through when he felt like it, passing on to the future. And where did that leave me except wishing that it was the *Empress of India* that was docked, not the old grey hulk that was taking them all away? And what could I do but wait for the sadness to turn into something else, standing there, watching time pass?

Hello, I said at last.

He turned then, blinded by the sun.

It's me, said I. Hello.

Agnes? He jumped to his feet, calling to a soldier nearby to keep an eye on his bundle. And he raced over to me and held me at arm's length to take a proper look.

It's not your war, said I, so why are you going?

Well, he took my hand without a word and led me quickly along the tracks, as if we had somewhere to go. And when we came to a pile of tea crates, he stopped and pushed me into the wedge of shade between them, pulled me tight to him, mouth and teeth. He was crazed now with haste, pulling the skirt up roughly and crouching to fit himself into me, grinding me back into the wood of the crate, no whisper of my name, no words at all, just the furious breath, and then the pause, and then the sigh.

A soldier stopped in front of the sun with his hands at his fly, looking in for a place to relieve himself. When he saw us, he laughed. Lucky bugger, said he, moving on.

And that's when the ship gave out a blast, and the men in the tavern stopped singing and sent up a roar. The hunter closed his eyes for a moment and laid his forehead against mine. You may not give a damn about it, Agnes, he said, but it's everyone's bloody war, you know.

31

WITH THE NEW BUILDINGS TO MY NAME, old and shabby as they were, I was mad to whip the hotel itself into shape. And so I had the staff polish the brass properly for once, and the silver too, and I myself mended the tablecloths and bought new material for the lounge curtains, which were perishing already in the sun. I ordered special ashtrays with "Railway Hotel" printed on them in green. And if the guests stole them, which they did, well I'd already increased the price of a room by the cost of two ashtrays and a face towel.

The place was fuller now than ever, with ships coming and going for supplies, and the wounded dropped off after a while, and fresh ones taken on. And there were wives sent from England to wait out the war, and their children too, that I couldn't, after all, refuse. And so the place was jollier than ever, with everyone wanting to cheer themselves up with a party and drinking.

The mother-in-law came often, bored to death with rolling bandages and serving soup to wounded soldiers at the Jewish Club. Sometimes we went up the coast for tea, and walked along the beach. And then she'd ask what had happened to the banker? And was I going to be running a hotel for the rest of my life? Agnes, said she, to grow old alone is to live the life of a dog.

But I'd been growing old alone since the day I was born, and there was no other way I could think of any more. If the Lord had intended a house and a husband for me, well it must have been the old Jew himself, and the house he'd hired me to keep for him. If I went upstairs now with one of the men staying at the hotel, it was because he had a way of looking at me that I liked. Nor was there a question of moving on into love, although for a day or two, I might have a quickening of the heart when I passed his door, a smile at the sight of him waiting for me at the bar. I was free, free of the terrible sickness and fright of love.

With the banker too, it was back to the way it had been before, except that now there was always a look when he dropped me off at the hotel, and a look again when he suggested a weekend down the coast, or a trip to the mountains.

If it were a story in a book, I would fall in love with him in the end, of course—the story of love is always in the search for it—and even if it was too late for him to love me back, still I'd come to know the foolishness of my own stubborn heart. But this wasn't a story, and there he was after a night at the pictures, saying, It's out of the question then, isn't it?

And I said, Yes, my dear, it's out of the question.

And after that he began staying away, only popping in for tea now and then. And I heard from the mother-in-law that he'd joined the Royal Club, and had asked her down with the husband for lunch one Sunday, but the husband had refused to go because no Jews could belong there, the members thought themselves too posh.

Well, I laughed then, because I didn't blame the husband, and I didn't blame the members either. They were always putting themselves above each other, one side and the other. And what would they have made of me if he took me there for lunch? And who did they think they were anyway?

I was teasing the banker with this over a cup of tea one day, when in burst Leah, pale and staring. Usually she came with Sarah, and then there was Sarah's nose lifting in the air, and her careful ways of keeping her clothes tight around her, as if there were fleas in the place, and even so the eyes were sliding off to notice how I'd done the flowers this week, or what was laid out for tea. And there was Leah at her side like a shadow, not wanting to lift the nose, but not wanting not to either.

Well, now there she was, collapsed onto the couch and sobbing, Ma! Ma!

For God's sake, said I, what's the matter?

And that's when she said, He's dead, he's dead.

And I thought the Japs must have shown up after all, except that there'd been no sirens and no bangs, and outside the traffic was coming and going as usual. And so I thought, He must have fallen off a cliff at the Bluff, and, Lord forgive me, I'm glad he's out of the way.

And I was about to say, I know how you feel, darling, but have a thought for Sarah, when she looked up, the face streaked with misery, and said, He was better than a real father to me, Ma.

And it took the banker to get my mind off that stupid tailor's dummy and on to the newspaperman, because he asked her, When did it happen? and, How?

He stepped on a mine, said she. And she covered her face with her hands.

Well, there was something about her grief that sent me off to the window to think of the newspaperman for myself. But I thought instead of the old Jew and the money he'd left me each time, the money he'd paid for the hotel, and for Leah too when he died. And as for the newspaperman, with his fingers hovering over the notes and coins in his palm, the care he'd always taken in counting out his owings on anything, well if she wanted to think of him as the real father, I wouldn't stop her. He'd come up with the name for her, and stalked up and down with the hands locked behind the back while she recited her spellings or a poem she'd learned by heart. He'd sat there as she sang, with his own eyes watery with love for the girl.

But real fathers had nothing to do with this sort of thing. They were there at the start, and there in what followed, body and soul, whether they liked it or not. And if they turned out wild and drunk, or quiet and loving, well it was too late to change the story around, too late right from the beginning.

32

1 9 4 5

WHEN THE WAR WAS OVER, SARAH AND the mother-in-law decided on a party in the big house to celebrate. Leah was sent backwards and forwards between them, to fetch tablecloths and glasses, and then down to the hotel with puddings to be kept in the big cold box.

She had spent the whole war up there on the ridge, like the children sent out from England, except that there I was down below, to be visited for tea, or when the newspaperman was blown to bits by a mine. And if she still had an eye for Sarah's husband, well there was no way of knowing it. Since she'd stopped taking money from me, or even coming down to have me run up a frock, she was beginning to look like a schoolteacher herself, or even a housekeeper, in the little white blouses and cheap cotton skirts, the pride all gone out of her somehow,

And did I want her back? No, I didn't. And yet even so, she was mine, and her sadness, if it was sadness, made me wild to shake it out of her. And when I saw her there on the night of the party, greeting the guests in the old green georgette, the shoes out of shape now, and the little string of glass beads I'd given her for winning that first bursary at the City Hall, well I wanted to take her over to the mirror right then and say, Look! Because there I was in my black chiffon, with the bodice beaded in jet, and the pearl earrings, and my hair loose and gleaming. And if the pinkness and the freshness was gone from me, then in its place was a sort of magnificence. I was forty-one years old and more alive, far more alive than this creature I'd given life to.

I took her by the arm and led her through to the lounge. The doors to the garden were wide open. Golden light poured out of the house, and the moon was full, and the trees all lit with fairy lights. People laughed, clinking their Champagne glasses. And the band played down in the summerhouse. Already, three couples were dancing on top of the air-raid shelter.

Look, said I, that's where you should be, down there, not standing in the hall like the housekeeper, taking hats and cloaks.

And that's when the mother-in-law came out to fetch her, wanting help in the kitchen, and asking me whether I'd mind cutting up the onion tart at the hors d'oeuvre table. She had made all her grandest dishes for the event—fish with mushrooms in pastry shells, cheese soufflés, honeyed loaves of bread, trifles, apple Charlotte, mango sherbet, even a platter of smoked salmon. And when everyone asked how she'd come by the salmon, well she just pretended not to hear, tapping her diamond ring to her ear.

But I knew the way she flirted with this one and that one for

a pair of nylon stockings, or real butter, or a passage on a ship for
one of her fenestrations. Getting what she wanted was a game
she played with life, and here she was now with the smoked
salmon and the nylon stockings and her passage booked to
America on the next ship out. And if she asked me to cut up an
onion tart, or to ice the puddings with whipped cream, well it
was always as a friend, never a servant. It was as if we understood the secret between us, she and I—the life we'd left
behind us, and the world we'd come into by our wits and our
beauty.

Sarah's husband was handsome as a Rajah in his bow tie
and tails, standing in the doorway as if he were about to make a
speech. When he saw me behind the hors d'oeuvre table, over
he came and bowed, and then made a great show of unbutton-
ing my glove so that he could kiss the skin of the wrist, and all
this because Sarah was nowhere to be seen.

Let me spirit you away for a dance, said he with a sly smile
and the voice to go with it. And even though the man's beauty
worked no magic on me, well I smiled back, letting him steer me
down the steps of the verandah, down through the rockeries to
the air-raid shelter below.

And, oh, it was lovely down there, dancing in the open air,
everyone turning to look at us, because there we were, a beautiful couple, one dark, one fair, and he an elegant dancer, and I
following without missing a step, as I'd done at his own wedding. And then the band went into my favorite tango, and it

was as if we were made for this, he and I, because they all cleared off to the sides and stood there watching, and oh, it was even better under the circle of eyes, and he no longer Sarah's husband, but every man in the world, and the pulse of the music like life itself.

And then, at last, it was over and he thought he had me for good, whispering into my ear that I was beautiful, he'd always thought me beautiful. But I laughed at him and shook his hand off my shoulder, pretending to have a cramp in the neck.

Coming up to the house, I saw the mother-in-law standing at the balustrade with the fancy man from the races. He steadied the glass in her hand, and then leaned over to say something into her ear, and I saw her look up and laugh, the diamonds all catching the light.

I stood still for a moment, stabbed with longing for such ordinary happiness, feeling like a cripple myself that I couldn't have it, and at the same time knowing I didn't even want it.

They saw me then, the two of them, and she came to the top of the steps and said, Agnes, I've been having such a laugh! And in we went together, leaving Sarah's husband and the fancy man behind, and there was Sarah, sitting on the couch, and Leah too, and a soldier between them with only one eye and a face and scalp all livid with scars. And when we passed, the soldier had to turn his head to watch us, and the mother-in-law whispered, Poor devil, one can only give thanks that it's not one's own.

And then a man behind me said, I see your daughter isn't trailing round in Mummy's dresses any more.

And when I turned, there was the tycoon, grinning like the devil himself, with a cigar between the teeth and the eyes bright as ever.

And although my heart was beating as if I'd just been grabbed by a madman, I said, So the war brought home the rats, did it?

And then the gleam hardened in the eyes and he stood back to examine the beading on my dress, the gloves and the earrings too. He looked over again at Leah and said, Surely you didn't come up with that outfit of hers, Agnes?

And he might as well have told me all over again that I needed new clothes myself, and manners to go with them, so cold did I feel for the girl, and wishing now I could change it all around, what I'd seen in that mirror, me and her. And how could I blame her for wanting what Sarah had come by so easily? And yet what did she think she was achieving in that old georgette, and the hair still up on the head although I'd told her it didn't suit her any more? She was plain and stupid and stubborn and proud, and I wished he were wrong but he wasn't.

And then one of Sarah's great-nephews came and led her out and down to the dance floor at last, and I followed, down into the garden to watch the dancing, with the tycoon behind me like the devil indeed.

Round and round they went under the fairy lights, Leah and

the great-nephew. There'd been no thought of going off to war for that family, certainly not. They'd stayed home to make money, and that's what he'd done, too. He was a bony dancer, shorter than she was, and with an awkward sort of ugliness. As for her, she was all airiness in the moonlight, graceful and smooth, and when a soldier cut in and took off with her into a waltz, and then another, well she laughed, the head thrown back and the hair coming loose from the pins. And, after all, there was nothing wrong with the green georgette, and the thick black curls were lovely all around the shoulders, the whole face flushed pink under the fairy lights.

The great-nephew cut back in and began pulling her towards the band. She laughed and pulled back, but he put on a show of pulling, and then up she went anyway, and there she settled herself next to the piano, and said something to the pianist, and then the band struck up "I'll Be Seeing You."

Well, everyone stopped talking then, as if "God Save the King" were playing.

Her face was lighted like an opal down there, and the arms held out before her, the voice clear and beautiful in the cool night air.

My God, said the tycoon, she's quite something, isn't she?

I moved away from him, to the edge of the rockery. And there was Sarah's husband, not even noticing that I stood beside him now. He gazed down at Leah as he'd gazed at his own child, the beautiful nostrils flaring, and the eyes watered over.

She was smiling as she sang, but there were tears streaming down her face. I looked at him. He had his hand to his throat and he closed his eyes.

On she went, as if she was really saying good-bye. I had never heard her sing any song like this before, but there she was now, beautiful, and the war was over, and she was every woman in the world, and every man's heart was with her.

33

AND THEN, BY THE NEXT MORNING, THE
whole town had the story of how Sarah found Leah and the
husband under the dark of the avocado pear tree. And how her
nails were out, and the voice booming for anyone to hear, and
Leah screaming, But it was only a kiss, Sarah! And the husband sliding off into the house through the back door.

When I went to fetch Leah, she was waiting at the gate with
her suitcases and boxes, and the scratches down her arms still
livid. All I could think was that she had crossed over now, she
had left them behind her at last. But when we were driving
through the racecourse and I suggested that she could make a
life for herself singing those songs, and a good life to go with it,
now that the war was over, well she said, Ma, can we just leave
it alone, please?

So we left it alone. And when we arrived at the hotel, old
Naidoo and the waiters were grinning all over the place to have
her back. And up she went to the double room I'd given her in
the corner upstairs, with an arrangement of hydrangeas, and a
bar of Vinolia, and a bottle of 4711.

And in the weeks and months that followed, the miracle was

that that kiss, if that's all it had been, seemed to turn her into a normal woman. There were phone calls now up in my sitting room, and a flush in the face when she came down afterwards. She didn't even mind the men around the bar any more. In fact, she would accept a drink from them on occasion, and ask them in a kind voice where they'd been in the war, and what they'd be doing now. I even heard her singing in the bath, popular songs that played on the wireless. And she wanted new dresses with lovely low necklines and skirts that showed off her hips as she walked.

She asked for the breakfast room at the back for her singing students, it would only be temporary, said she, until she could take up the bursary. And there was none of the usual tightness and pride when she wanted something from me, waiting for my answer as if it made all the difference in the world, and no difference at all either. So, of course, I had to join in the spirit of the thing, and say it was no hardship in the least, she could have the room as long as she liked. And out went the table and chairs and in went a new little piano she'd bought with her own money. And even so, she wasn't always waiting for a chance to get at that piano. She sat in the lounge musing, with a little smile on the face, and when I said, A penny for your thoughts, she just shook her head and shrugged.

Well, I felt a fool, playing this little game, but what could I do? She was gone most of the day, and at night it was up in her room, or off with the great-nephew. Since that party, she had him madly in love with her too. And even though anyone could see she wasn't in love with him—the little fox face, and the black hair curling on the knuckles—still she didn't seem to mind going to the pictures with him or even dinner-dancing.

And if it was Sarah's husband she'd got hold of after all, well she took care to roll the eyes or even curl the lips in a sneer at the mention of his name. But still I wanted to warn her, I wanted to shake her out of it. It seemed like a waste, all this life in her at last and him taking the best of it for himself. But what could I do to pull her out of her hiding place?

What's the news of the bursary? said I. And, What do the Jews think of that great-nephew in love with his great-aunt?

Well, she wouldn't budge. England was a mess at the moment, said she. She wanted to wait till things settled down a bit there. And as for the great-nephew, she just laughed. She even put an arm around me and said, Ma, don't be such an old hen!

Well, she was right. With her back in the hotel, I was turning into an old hen. For all the life in her, she was more of a stranger to me now than the day she'd been born, a grown woman with a grown woman's secrets.

And yet, she herself felt quite at home. She had the double room to herself, and the motorcar whenever she needed it. And somehow, it was as if the hotel suited her at last. But, as for myself, I couldn't stand the pleasant little smile when she came down for tea, or the humming off upstairs to make a telephone call, with the bottom thrusting from side to side as she walked, so that the men at the bar went mad with whistling.

She'd even had her hair cut soft around the face, with a side parting and a little clip. And the clothes weren't girlish any more either, but sleek and well cut in the best materials. She used her own money to hire Sarah's dressmaker after all, a little Coloured woman who came to the hotel for fittings. And there was laughing in the music room now, and then the dressmaker came through with the bare gums grinning, and, What a lovely daughter you got, Missus! said she. And for a while I even wondered whether the tycoon might have a hand in all this. But when I mentioned his name, Leah frowned, remembering him only as the reason we'd had to leave the Avondale. So it wasn't him.

Of all the secrets she'd kept, this one got on my nerves the most. It wasn't that I wanted what she had, or that I wanted to take it away from her either. It was myself I couldn't stand, the thin little smile I wore myself when she came down for tea, me wondering where she'd been all the morning, and wanting to ask, although at the same time I wanted her to know that I couldn't care less. And, in fact, I couldn't.

It was my own life that seemed as dull as any woman's now. Even the mother-in-law had become so wild in her daring that word got out she had a fancy man in town. And then both sons had called at his office and told him to leave their mother alone or there'd be trouble, they even threatened to give him a hiding. And all this she told me with the eyes bright with the drama of it all.

She herself had been thrilled by all the fuss about Leah and

Sarah's husband under the avocado pear tree. Sarah had it coming, said she, down there at the theater morning to night, and not even baking the man his favorite biscuits, as if she could bake at all, which she couldn't to save her life. And now the mother-in-law was off to America for a fenestration, and even my old banker was packing up and going back to England, where he belonged.

As for me, when I looked in the mirror now, I felt indeed like a bit of an old hen. And the funny thing was that I couldn't remember how it had been before, sauntering down the street or along the docks. It was a problem of seeing. Once you saw the old hen, then the magnificence melted away and there was the knowledge that you couldn't bring it back just by wanting to. And the more you wanted, the more of an old hen you were. And it was as if you'd always known you'd turn into an old hen, but that the turning had been so slow as to slip by your notice. And then along came someone like Leah who could make you see the difference.

And so I took to staying out of her way. I would sit on the upstairs verandah for a sundowner, staring across at the rick-shaw rank and the natives swarming out of the station, and the schoolgirls in their Panama hats, and I thought, They all love someone, even the natives. In my story it's different. There's only me. I knew that, I'd known it all along. But suddenly the past seemed like the past, and the present like the future. So where did that leave me now?

34

AND THEN, ONE AFTERNOON, SARAH BURST INTO THE hotel. She pushed her way past me in the hall. Where is she? she cried. Is she up there?

She took to the stairs, pulling herself up by the banister, two at a time, and then pausing at the top, the bosom heaving. Which way? she said.

If you mean Leah, said I, she's out. But I went down the passage anyway, and knocked at the door, and tried the handle, with Sarah breathing like a dragon behind me. Then I pulled out my keys and found the one. And of course the room was empty, with Leah's things all neatly arranged on the dressing table, brush and comb, lipsticks and rouge, the flannel drying on the basin, and the toothbrush and paste in the mug. It seemed so normal, everything there in order, that I said, What's the fuss about now?

She didn't answer, just made for the wardrobe and pulled open the doors, as if she'd find the girl hiding in there. Agnes, said she, I need your help. *Please!* she cried fiercely, as if I'd refused.

But I hadn't refused. I'd only gone to get the wicker chair so that she could sit down. The skin was pale as milk and the eyes red, and when she caught sight of herself in the wardrobe mirror, she turned away to scrabble in the handbag for a cigarette, and then flicked furiously at it with the lighter. I'll wait here until she returns, said she, sitting down at last.

Any minute, I thought, she'll be saying, Like mother like daughter. And she'd be right and she'd be wrong too. I would never have lasted all those years, mooning like a dog over such a man, never.

What's going on? said I.

Well, she looked up then with a dreadful smile, and she might as well have said, Like mother like daughter, after all, because there it was all over her face. And even so, I felt sorry for her, so small and ugly and left behind, the way she'd always been.

She'll never be able to keep him, Sarah, said I. He'll break her heart, if it's any consolation.

Consolation! she cried. As if I need consolation from *you*! Ghugh!

Anyway, said I, they all go a bit funny in the war, you know, even out there on the Bluff.

The *war?* she boomed, sitting forward as if to spit. He didn't give a tinker's cuss for the war! She was breathing hard now, never taking the eyes off me. And then she gave the horrible thin little smile. Like mother like daughter! she spat out at last.

Well, I just smiled too, a saucy old smile that got on her nerves, even though there was an emptiness in my heart for her,

I couldn't help it. She seemed marooned up there in her house on the hill, trying to look in every direction while enemies slipped in under the door. And down here was Leah singing in the bath, and me with another building at the docks. And even if I felt like an old hen, well she didn't know it and I wouldn't tell her either.

And just when I thought she'd come over and have a go at me with the nails, well she just shivered and said, To think that I kept that creature under my wing like a viper for all those six years.

If it had been a story in a book, I would have had a go at her myself to defend my own child. I would have found a way to blame her for the husband she herself had chosen. But there she was now, every bit as miserable as the day I'd first met her. And certainly she'd lose this man too, not to Leah, but to some other woman, and then to another, and then another. And how could I tell her that it wouldn't matter a jot, she'd hardly even notice he was gone before he'd be back again, he was that sort of man? And that she'd never really had him in the first place? She'd never really had anyone, not even her own father.

She sighed and sat back, crossed the legs, smoothed down the stockings. It comes from my side of the family, you know, said she. My grandfather was a cantor, one of my aunts used to sing too.

And so there we were like a pair of ladies having tea again, while she took all the good things in the girl for her side and left the slut for me.

It's a damned waste of talent, she said, when you think of what she might have become.

And so I said, The story isn't over yet, Sarah, you mark my words.

And that's when I heard the front door bang, and Leah's hello to Naidoo. Sarah lifted her chin and took a deep breath, as if she were about to sing herself. And, oh Lord, I thought, they'll be putting it on for each other now. It's the old Jew they're fighting over, the past and the future, and, yes, I did want Leah to win. I was mad for her to win this time.

35

LEAH MUST HAVE SEEN THE MOTORCAR outside because, by the time she opened the door, there was a false little smile on her face. She walked straight past Sarah and over to me. Hello, Ma, said she, how are you?

Well, I knew she was putting it on. She never asked me how I was in case I might tell her. I could fall through a window, and all she'd say was, Do you want a cup of tea, Ma? keeping herself as far as possible from the fuss. But here she was now, bending over me for a kiss on the cheek.

Come off it, said I, you and your stupid little secrets!

Well, she just sauntered over to the basin then, and took her time rinsing out the mug and filling it up again, drying underneath it with a towel. She looked at herself in the mirror and began to sip the water.

Sarah stood up, the arms folded and the nails digging into her own flesh now. *What do you have to say for yourself?* she demanded.

But Leah just sipped on.

I know what's happened, said Sarah, poking the whole face forward like a dagger.

So?

So? So? boomed Sarah. Is that all you have to say? So?

That's all, said Leah. But for all the performance she was putting on, the chin held high and the eyelids drooping, she had to use one hand to hold the other steady.

Sarah grabbed for the chair and fell back into it. Where were you meeting? she whispered.

Leah shrugged. She was even beautiful now, the way she was standing there, tall and haughty, with the lovely bosom and the hips round under the flimsy stuff of the sundress.

Sometimes we took the gramophone down to the beachfront, she said.

What gramophone? cried Sarah.

But Leah pressed her lips together and shook her head. The chin quivered a bit now and the eyes were closed. It's being taken care of, said she.

Taken care of? said I, sitting up myself. What's to be taken care of, may I ask?

What do you think? mumbled Leah.

Well, I looked at her then, the face and the figure, nothing beautiful about them all of a sudden, nothing at all. So, you'll do the bidding of that tailor's dummy? said I. Or is this your idea too?

Tailor's dummy! cried Sarah. Ha! *Tailor's dummy!*

There's someone down at the docks, mumbled Leah, all the swagger gone out of her. I thought you'd help me, Ma.

Well, Sarah poked herself forward again. I suppose you

thought you'd get him away from me by falling pregnant? said she. Huh?

I'll be going to London when it's over, mumbled Leah. The bursary's all arranged. You'll never have to see me again, anyone.

And that's when I stood up. Excuse me, said I, just excuse *me* a minute! If you think a little bleeding, a little pain will wipe away what's happened, well you'll have washed away the only thing alive in you except the singing and the bit of love you found by it at last.

She looked up, the dark eyes fixed on me now.

One day you'll be an old woman, my girl, said I, an old hen yourself, and who knows what regrets you'll be carrying, like a witch's burden, over your shoulder then?

Oh Ma! she cried. She came over to me and held on tight, weeping pitifully.

Agnes! cried Sarah, leaping to her feet. What the *hell* do you think you're doing?

Well, I unfolded the girl and stepped forward myself.

And just *who* do you think you are to be asking me the same stupid question in a hundred different ways over all these years? I hope you realize, Agnes? and, Have you ever considered, Agnes? Well, what the *hell* do *you* know about love, for all the parts you've played? You're a sad and ugly little thing yourself, and nothing will ever change that.

She opened the mouth then, but on I went.

You listen to me, you stupid cow. You'll never be safe from me. I'll be there like a ghost every time you look in the mirror, in the past and in the future now, too.

And I would have carried on, except that she was halfway to the stairs already, and me hanging over the banisters, shouting on, and the whole hotel listening.

And then after she'd gone, I went onto the upstairs verandah, and looked out on the life of the street, the words we'd said going through my head like a love song, and Leah's crying too, even the sight of Sarah flying down the stairs, running for her life.

36

AND THAT'S HOW I CAME TO BE MOTHER TO Leah's daughter, Bess. She was a beautiful child, dark like the father, but wilful like me, and rosy too. And how had I thought I'd ever loved another creature until now?

She was like a joke on myself, everything upside down in my life, so that it was she I had in mind when I stood before the wardrobe, choosing what to wear, or at the butcher, or the fishmonger, or collecting the rent for my buildings. When I dressed, there she was, dancing beside me in the mirror, loving herself as I loved her.

Three days after the birth, Leah had signed the papers, the child was mine. And then, three weeks later, off Leah went to London. And now, every week there was a letter from her, very dull with the talk of rehearsals and the cold, the boots she'd had to buy, and thank you for the money. And just when I thought she would never amount to much, creeping around London in the rain, well then a letter arrived to say she had sung at Covent Garden, the real singer had caught a cold. And after that, in came the newspaper clippings, and then the new address in Mayfair, trips to the Continent, too. I took the clippings down

Marine Hotel

to the morning paper, and added a few things of my own to cheer up the story a bit. And so now the whole town knew that Allegra La Grange had amounted to something in the world, with a house in the country, and summers spent in France.

Meanwhile, the Municipal Corporation decided to buy up the Railway Hotel for the new post office after all. They gave me eighteen months and a fair price too, and just when I was thinking I'd have to buy a house of my own whether I liked it or not, well then the old Marine Hotel had a fire, and no one but me seemed willing to redo it. And so, by the time Bess was four years old, there was my lovely hotel on the corner, rising up like a wedding cake from the bay, with its pillared verandahs, and the ships sailing past, and the band playing every afternoon for tea.

Bess and I had the top floor, with ceiling fans for the heat, and coir matting on the floors, and, oh, it was lovely to sit out on our own little verandah in the evenings, looking at the ships passing so close that the sailors could wave to us from the deck, and we could wave back. There were yachts passing, too, and rowing boats that tied up at the bottom of the steps. Every afternoon, we walked out along the Esplanade, she and I, and then down along to the docks. And there, with the smell of the fish and the whales, and the Coloured girls in their high heels and bangles, and the sailors gathered around them, well we were both bright with life.

With the child at my side, the Coloured girls hardly noticed me any more, even though the men themselves might look and I might smile back. There is nothing about a child to keep a woman from a man, although the sailors seemed like boys to me now, and I didn't need so much to be catching their eye.

And then, one day, the bar waiter came in with a letter, holding it by one corner because the envelope was crumpled and dirty, torn at the edges. A native from the north had brought this, said he, and he was waiting for an answer.

I tore open the envelope.

19 January, 1941. Agnes, if you receive this note, I didn't make it back from the war. Please do what you can for the bearer. He is half mine, after all, as I've always been half yours, in my own way——

I read the words again and again. But even though he was dead, long dead, his words seemed alive in my hand. I folded them up again, and went down to the kitchen, with Bess following behind me.

There he stood, a light-skinned native boy of nineteen or twenty, with the hunter's deep eyes and fierce chin. For the rest, he seemed like all the others, looking down at the bare feet, the hands clasped before him like a servant.

I knew you as a small boy, said I, and Bess looked up to see if I was joking. She even laughed.

He reached quickly into his satchel then and pulled out a packet, gave it to me with both hands. From my mother, said he.

And, of course, it was another little beaded purse on a beaded string. Bess reached up for it, and so I hung it around her neck, took a penny from my own to put into it. And oh, the sight of it there, and the boy's shy smile—well I turned away, suffering a terrible loneliness. And somehow Bess knew this, because she pulled the purse off and held it out to me again. And what could I do then but lift her into my arms, the smell of her like sweet milk custard, and kiss the face and the hair, tears streaming down my own cheeks now so that the boy shuffled backwards in embarrassment.

Well, I couldn't put him to work with the native staff, or with the Indians either. To them, he was a Coloured boy, and to me the hunter's son. So he hung about on his own for those first few weeks with a broom in his hand, propping it against the wall whenever he could and looking out over the bay. He was homesick, anyone could see that, even Bess. She drew pictures for him and made little gifts. And the only time I saw him smile was when she played with him.

One day, the mother-in-law noticed him with the child and asked why I let her play with a Coloured boy. And so I told her who he was and why he'd come, and she took a good look at him then, saying she'd try him out as a garden boy if I liked, the new one she'd hired was a drinker. But I shook my head. He'd stay with me as the hunter had wanted, at least until he had the courage to pack up his things and take off one night without warning, making his way back home.

She took a lollipop out of her bag to lure the child to her. She came to us secretly, Bess and me, leaving her car and driver around the corner. The husband was still outraged at the thought of the child born without his permission. And yet the child was so beautifully hers, more than the rest of them, some-how, and we ourselves more like sisters now than friends. Every Wednesday afternoon, when the nanny was off and the hus-band playing bowls, the mother-in-law took Bess shopping. And back they would come with stories of what Bess had done and what she had said, and Bess wearing a new ribbon, or a tiny muff.

And then one day, without warning, the mother-in-law took her to Sarah's for the afternoon. And the next day Sarah rang me up on the telephone and said, Perhaps, for the sake of the girl, it would be an idea if we had tea once in a while?

Well, I hadn't seen Sarah since that day she'd burst into the Railway Hotel. And now there she was, out on the old veran-dah pouring tea, and Bess off climbing trees in the garden with her youngest daughter, not a year older than herself.

They know nothing of who she is, of course, said Sarah in a low voice. She was a handsome woman now, strapped into a corset, with the milk-white skin, and the scarlet lips and the scarlet nails to match.

I smiled at her. What the girls knew or didn't know had nothing to do with either of us. They were sisters twice over, these children, and I'd tell Bess the truth when she wanted to hear it, Sarah or no Sarah.

Just as well they're both girls, hey? said the mother-in-law, laughing like a drain.

Sarah's husband himself had arrived at the hotel once, ask-ing for a look at the baby. He'd stood in the lounge, looking around like a spy, to see who might have noticed him come in. And then, once he saw her, the eyes watered up and he reached out for her, held her to him and said, Oh Agnes, I'd like to be more than a stranger to her.

But I only folded my arms and shook my head. If he'd had his way, she'd have been taken care of and down the drain before she was anything at all. Certainly, she was his, everything about her. But so what? It was not by choice, and not by law either. She was Bess La Grange, and I myself her mother and her father now.

And then, sure enough, when she was old enough to wonder, she asked about her father, who he was, and where, and how. And so I told her the whole story, and the funny thing was that, for all his beauty and his fancy ways, it wasn't him she wanted to know about at all, it was Leah. Over and over she wanted the story of the old sewing tin, and the ga-ga looks she'd given him after the concerts. And when I put on the ga-ga look myself, she'd laugh like a fishwife, holding her sides and cackling. And when I told her about the party, and Leah singing "I'll Be Seeing You," and him up there with his mouth hanging open, and the nails and the shouting under the avocado pear tree, and Sarah storming in and opening the wardrobe doors, looking for the culprit, well then she'd hold a hand to her mouth and gasp. But I never told her that they'd wanted her taken care of, and I never let him come back to see her again.

37

AND THEN, WHEN BESS WAS SEVENTEEN, Leah came home for her first visit. There she was, poised at the top of the gangway, tall and handsome and serious under a large black hat. And when she came down step by step, with the photographers from both newspapers squatting for a shot and a reporter asking her questions, well then suddenly I saw Bess, her eyes fiery as a Spaniard's, bewitched by the idea of such a mother.

Leah came to stand before her, the newspaper people following.

Hello, Bess, said she, I've been trying to imagine this for years. And of course that was the picture both papers chose to put in: Allegra La Grange greets her sister Bess La Grange.

And after that, the girl was never the same. She followed Leah like a great leaping dog, down to breakfast and up to the room, watching while she dressed, and then down again to the verandah for tea with Sarah.

She's a credit to you, Agnes, said Sarah, when the girl had gone off for a plate of cakes. And Leah nodded, looking out over the bay. But I needed no credit from Sarah or from anyone else, for that matter. I watched Bess as I might watch myself. I listened for her voice calling all over the hotel, the school shoes flung across the room so that she could run barefoot along the passages to find me. I watched her toss her lovely head if the wrong man whistled, saw her fix her eyes on the ones she wanted, staring straight back without a smile, nothing coy about her. And when we went to the pictures and watched the stories of girls taken up by dukes and princes, girls going across the ocean in ships, well then she was brilliant with longing. And it didn't matter at all that I'd had little as a girl, and she had everything at her feet for the taking. She was after adventure, my Bess, not a suite in a hotel and a game of hockey on a hot afternoon.

So there we sat now—Sarah almost sixty, and Leah's hair dyed into streaks of brown and blonde that didn't suit her at all. I myself was stiff in the joints, with my thick grey hair swirled up into a bun. And then out came Bess with the plate of cakes, and how could I tell her that Leah had been born to what she was, solid and true, but that she, Bess, was light as air, there'd be nothing to take with her but the dream she had of what she was going to, the ending of a story, which was no ending at all, because even if a duke or a prince did come to save her, still he would want something back, and what did she have to give but her youth and beauty, which would come to nothing in the end?

And then, three weeks later, the night before she left, Leah knocked at my door. She came and sat in an armchair, and said, It's not the great life you may think it is, Ma.

I looked up, because somehow I'd known this all along. The old pride was gone out of the eyes, and the mouth a little bitter at the edges.

I've never really made it to the top, said she. I didn't have it in me to make it to the top.

Well, I looked away because her eyes were watering over now and she'd never been one to enjoy a cry. Still I could see her in the old mirror, a middle-aged woman who would never make it to the top, and there was such joy in my heart with the knowledge, my Bess safe from her somehow, that I had to get up and go over to the liquor cabinet for a whiskey and soda, and one for her as well.

Do you want to come home? I asked, knowing she would shake her head, which she did.

Look at Sarah, said she bitterly. I could have been like that, teaching pupils in that little theater year after year. She smoothed down the skirt with a sigh.

And then, somehow, I knew what she would say before she said it, and my breath stopped in my throat.

That money from my father, she said, I'm going to give it to Bess.

I have money for Bess myself, I whispered.

Well, I want her to have his too, she said.

I put down the glasses of whiskey. Don't tell her, I begged. Keep it a secret, at least for now.

She leaned forward then and said, But I told her already, Ma.

And already the hotel seemed enormous to me, the whole empty weight of it filling up the future. I looked at Leah and she tried a smile, but it didn't work. Her suitcases were packed and ready in her room. She'd go back to her life on that ledge, halfway to the top, but what about my Bess with her dreams and her wildness?

She's just finished school, said I. She'd do better to be a housekeeper to an old man herself, a girl in the circus—

Leah smiled, her old careful smile. Oh Ma, she said, that's your life, not hers.

38

1 9 8 6

I'VE ALWAYS LIKED THE END OF A STORY. When I read a book, I read the ending first to see if I can bear to make the journey, page after page. Well, I am an old woman now, thick in the hips and the ankles, and the skin dry as tissue paper. I walk with a stick and live at the Majestic. When Bess ran off and the Marine burned down for the last time, well I gave up on the great future then.

The whole town knows my story. I see them glance at each other, standing aside to let me pass. Every five years or so, someone comes from the newspaper to ask me to tell it again. They think it's a matter of luck, these stupid young oafs, as if an old woman is like a wishing well. They think it's a story about money. But if I had to tell them the truth, I'd tell them that before the money, there was the faith in what the money would bring, and never an end to the journey either.

I sold the Marine two weeks before it caught fire. I sold the buildings down at the docks as well. And now all my money's in the Building Society, and the new owners have nothing, not even insurance. And so, there's luck in it after all, I suppose, if I wanted to feel lucky, an old woman with her life behind her and a purse around her neck.

When I look in the mirror now, I see the girl I was before ever I'd seen her that first time in the old Jew's attic. All day I remember her, backwards and forwards, right up to the time the ship left Southampton. It's better than a story in a book because I know what follows and she doesn't. She's a strange sort of girl with a superior set of the mouth, always standing aside as if she might slip out through the door and never come back. Which is what she did anyway.

They watch me in the lounge or in the dining room, the other residents, and think I'm longing for my daughter and for her daughter, too. But they are wrong. It is myself I am with day and night, even in my dreams. I see the whole story written in the girl that I once was, what she would come to and how she would get there too. Perhaps that is what I'd loved so dearly in my Bess, the way she watched and listened for a chance to move on, out into the great world.

Well, there she is now in her little house outside London, and a husband and a life to go with it. I keep her letters in a box, as she's asked me to, but I never read them twice. She'll have the money that she wants so badly, of course, but it will never be to her what it was to me. She'll turn it into fancy things and trips to the Continent, all the hope gone out of it somehow.

After breakfast, I take my stick and go out along the Esplanade. If it's a fine day, and not too hot, I walk all the way to the docks, and there I find a bench under a palm and settle down for a half hour or so of thinking. The whales are gone now, and there are fences up to keep smugglers away from the ships. I'm invisible to the Coloured girls, and to the sailors too, an old woman with a stick sitting on a bench. Only the natives notice me, wondering why I'm there and whether they might do me a favor for a coin.

If there's anyone I think of, it's Sarah, the girl who opened that door to me all those years ago. And that booming voice of hers, oh Lord, that voice. When I hear it now on the wireless or over the telephone, what I see is myself and my cardboard suitcase, not standing on the top step of that house, waiting for her to let me in, but waiting on the dock at Southampton, touching the purse around my neck to make sure it was still there.

Everything is at a distance now except the girl I'd been before. A few years ago, I took a holiday on a ship, sailing around the bottom of Africa, and then sailing back again on another, thinking that the journey might bring that girl further still. But it didn't. She had come to this place to make her way in the world, and there was no need for me to bring her back again.

Grateful acknowledgment is made to the following for permission to reprint photographs:

Local History Museums' Collection, Durban
Title page (rickshaw driver), pages 6, 10, 18, 29, 43, 77, 83, 103, 111, 121, 159

The Royal Hotel, Durban
pages 40, 115, 137, 207

Killie Campbell Africana Library
page 178

Other photographs are courtesy of the author

Caption calligraphy by William Lung.

About the Author

LYNN FREED was born and grew up in Durban, South Africa, where two of her previous novels—*Home Ground* and *The Bungalow*—are set. Ms. Freed's stories and essays have appeared in *The New Yorker, Harper's, Story,* the *New York Times,* the *Washington Post,* and elsewhere. She lives in Sonoma, California.